Christmastime 1940

A Love Story

LINDA MAHKOVEC

Other Books by Linda Mahkovec

The Dreams of Youth

Seven Tales of Love

The Garden House

The Christmastime Series

Christmastime 1941: A Love Story

Christmastime 1942: A Love Story

Christmastime 1943: A Love Story

Christmastime 1940: A Love Story
by Linda Mahkovec

...

Copyright © 2012

ISBN-10:1-946229-05-9
ISBN-13:978-1-946229-05-2

Distributed by Bublish, Inc.

Cover Design by Laura Duffy
© Colin Young/Dreamstime

To lovers and merrymakers everywhere –
and, as always,
to my mother,
Agnes Mandeville Mahkovtz.

Chapter 1

◦ᢒ

The first light of morning revealed a heavy sky over Manhattan, dappled clouds that promised snow. A few early risers looked forward to the first snowfall of the season, hoping it would last until Christmas.

Shop owners, as they unlocked their stores or rolled down their awnings, wondered how it would affect business. They hoped this holiday season would be profitable, despite the news from Europe.

For others, the threat of snow intensified the sense of unease that was now a part of daily life. As they stopped at the newsstands for their morning papers, they read the headlines with the now familiar foreign words: "Luftwaffe," "Blitz," "Führer."

Some of the veterans could feel it in the old wounds that never really healed – war was coming sure as winter was coming. They shuddered that it could be happening again, and thought of the brothers lost, the limbs lost, the minds forever scarred. They shook their heads as they walked or limped away with their newspapers.

Mothers read the headlines and heard the dire news on the radio and bit their nails, or smoothed the brows of their little ones as they watched them sleep, calculating how many years before their sons could be torn from them.

One such mother, the widow Lillian Hapsey, parted the curtains in her sons' bedroom, allowing the morning light to gently nudge her boys away from dreamland.

"Time to get up," she said softly.

As expected, they mumbled a few sounds of protest and rolled over. Lillian leaned down and kissed their foreheads, smoothing back their hair. She gave them a few more minutes to cross from night to day, from sleep to waking, while she went to her room and dressed for work.

Lillian looked in the mirror above her vanity and, for the first time in years, wondered how she would appear to a stranger. How might a handsome man find her – plain? Worn, even? She stood in profile, then stepped closer to the mirror, and frowned at the tiny lines around her eyes and mouth.

She browsed through her closet, and on impulse pulled out her blue silk dress with the tiny white polka dots and white collar and cuffs – her special occasion dress. She tilted her head, trying to remember when she had last worn it. A wedding, two years ago – or was it three?

She held up the dress against her and glanced at her reflection, thinking she might as well get some use out of it. It would be nice to feel attractive again – not that she was looking for anyone, far from it. But in that moment, she decided that she wanted prettiness back in her life – and just like that, a tiny door opened up inside her, and a thin thread of connection was cast out into the world.

She slid the dress over her slip, and sat at the vanity to fasten her stockings. Then she clipped on her pearl earrings, applied some lipstick, and looked at herself in the mirror again, satisfied that she looked just a little bit new and different. This was to be a fresh beginning, after all.

She went back to the boys' room, turned on the light, and spoke in a louder voice.

"Tommy, Gabriel, time to get up for school."

She jostled them lightly. "It looks like it might snow today."

Her words had the effect she was hoping for, and after a few disoriented seconds of remembering that they were in their new home, the boys jumped out of bed and ran to the window, searching in vain for the snowflakes that might allow them a snow day from school.

"Yippee! Snow today!" Gabriel craned his neck to see the sky. He then dashed out of his bedroom and headed to the bathroom.

"Me first!"

"Not if I get there before you!" said Tommy, pushing past him.

Lillian listened to the sounds of water splashing and drawers opening and closing, relieved that the boys hadn't gone back to bed. While they washed and dressed for school, she lit the stove for the coffee pot, and filled a pan of water to boil. She opened the bread drawer and took out the bakery loaf, giving it a quick squeeze. Still soft.

She buttered one slice to go with her coffee, and used the rest to make peanut butter and jam sandwiches for their lunches. Then she wrapped them in wax paper and put the boys' sandwiches in their Hopalong Cassidy and Lone Ranger lunchboxes, and placed hers in a paper bag. She added apples and two sugar cookies each for the boys.

The water in the pan was now popping and splashing. She lowered the flame and stirred oatmeal into the pan. The rich aroma from the coffee rose and filled the cold morning kitchen; it was a small moment but one of her favorites of the day. She poured herself a cup, and inhaled deeply before taking that first, heavenly sip.

As she waited for the oatmeal to thicken, she took her coffee and opened the curtains by the kitchen table. On the street below, she saw the milkman delivering bottles to the stoops. Not so unlike their old home in Brooklyn. She imagined mothers skimming the cream for their husbands' coffee, or pouring milk for their children's cereal.

Lillian warmed her hands around the cup and blew lightly on the steaming coffee. Up and down the street she noticed a few early signs of Christmas: red ribbons and garlands of pine boughs twisted around some of the brownstone balustrades, and a few wreaths already decorated the doors and windows.

She was grateful for the cheer and hope of the merrymakers that helped to diminish the encroaching gloom that increasingly filled the newspapers. This was their first Christmas in their new home, and it had to be a good one.

She needed this change, she thought, as she stirred the oatmeal. She had grown tired of herself, and had forced herself to climb out of her apathy, find a new job, a new apartment, and learn to live again.

Her friend Izzy had recommended the area west of Central Park, and something about this street had charmed her from the first time she saw it – the way the elms reached across both sides to form a canopy of branches, the familiarity of the brownstones, the tranquility of the street so near the bustle of the city. Or maybe she was just seeing what she wanted to see – something beautiful, promising, lifting.

Her thoughts wandered to her neighbor down the hall, Drooms was the name on his mailbox, and how she had met him the day she moved in, nearly three weeks ago.

She had come upon him suddenly as she turned up the stairs. He was just coming down the third floor hall, and for the briefest of moments, they stood staring at one another. For those few seconds, she had felt a profound connection to him, something beyond attraction, though she had been struck by his handsome face and broad shoulders. She briefly introduced herself, but he had simply stepped aside for her and the boys to pass, never saying a word. She thought she caught a glimpse of something in his face, some recognition of – what, was it really something or just her imagination?

No, she decided, as she poured the oatmeal into bowls, she must have been mistaken. For ever since that day, he seemed to have no interest in her whatsoever; she even felt that he was avoiding her. And just as well. She had no time for such things, and certainly didn't desire any further connection.

Still, she couldn't help wondering about him. She had seen him on another occasion, coming home with a package tied in red string. At the time, she thought it must be something for his wife, but had later been told he was a bachelor. Since then, they had only passed each other now and then. He seemed to be a rather crabby, irascible kind of man. She hoped he wasn't going to be difficult. At any rate, this was their new home, and she would be as neighborly to him as to all the other tenants.

She sprinkled brown sugar on top of the oatmeal, just as the boys clamored into their seats, discussing what they would do when it snowed.

"I'm going to build a snow fort," said Gabriel, taking a spoonful of oatmeal.

Tommy shook his head. "There's not enough room for that. But we could make a barricade and stock it with snowballs."

"Yeah, we'll make a barricade," said Gabriel, who agreed with Tommy ninety percent of the time.

Lillian rested her eyes on them, thinking how quickly they were growing up. At nine years old, Tommy was already starting to get more angular, leaner, leaving little boyhood behind him. Even his expressions were subtly changing – sometimes now, he smiled with just one side of his mouth, especially when something made him a little shy or self-conscious, and at other times he had a way of cocking his head back to the side in a challenging manner.

And Gabriel – at six he was still all sweetness and softness, though he could hold his own against Tommy. She wondered if he would outgrow his curls, as Tommy had.

Both boys raised their heads.

"What?" said Tommy.

"What are you looking at, Mommy?" asked Gabriel.

"Oh, nothing. Finish your oatmeal." She rinsed the coffee pot and set their lunches on the table by the door.

Ten minutes later, they were pulling on their coats and hats. Except for Gabriel's shoes being on the wrong feet, the boys were ready to go. Such trouble-free mornings were rare, and Lillian hoped that, in part, it meant the boys were happy about the new place. It made her feel more confident that she had made the right decision to move. With a swish of her blue dress as she put on her coat, it was with a lightness of heart that she left her apartment with the boys in tow.

*

Just a few moments ahead of her, from the same brownstone apartment building, Old Man Drooms left for work. At forty-five he was hardly old, but that's what the neighborhood children called him, for he somehow had the feel of an old man.

And it suited him just fine.

He had long ago adopted the mask of a curmudgeon to keep the busybodies away. Dressed in a long gray coat and gray hat, he always walked with his head bent down, his shoulders slightly hunched. As another person might wrap their scarf or turn up their collar to keep out the cold, Drooms kept out the world by keeping his head down and his mind focused on work.

However, on this particular morning, a cheerful female voice threatened to break through his façade as he walked down the sidewalk.

"Good morning, Mr. Drooms!" called Lillian, coming out of the brownstone.

He almost turned around, but his long practice of ignoring such remarks served him well and he continued on, a slight flinch the only indication that he had heard her.

Drooms frowned as he remembered the day she moved in. He had been leaving for work as usual, but had to step aside as two rambunctious boys stormed up the stairs, and all of a sudden – there she was – on the landing below him, looking up. Why he had stopped and stared, he couldn't say. For one split second he had let down his guard, and she had slipped through a chink in his walled exterior.

He must have been distracted or tired or something, he now thought with annoyance. Well, there would be no more such slips. That was already three weeks ago. She should have learned to avoid him by now. Maybe she was one of those dull, pretty women who had to have everything spelled out for her. He turned up his collar and directed his thoughts to work.

*

Lillian was beautiful and brisk – and young, in the same way that Drooms was old, though only ten years separated them in age. On most days, Lillian moved with a supple, light energy, no doubt, in part, to keep up with her boys.

Tommy and Gabriel were now several steps ahead of her on their way to the home of Mrs. Kuntzman, the babysitter on the corner who would later walk them to school. They saw her standing at the door of her brownstone, waiting to welcome them. She was in her late sixties, gray-haired and a bit stooped, and utterly grandmotherly in her affection for Tommy and Gabriel. Even though Lillian had told her it wasn't necessary, she often had pancakes or cobbler or some other treat freshly made for the boys.

Tommy ran up the stairs, with Gabriel trailing behind calling, "Wait for me!"

Though Lillian had tried to smooth down Tommy's cowlick and Gabriel's curls, their hair still looked tousled from sleep. As they said goodbye, the vulnerability in their sweet faces squeezed her heart, as it did every day. She waited for them to go inside, where they always knocked on the window and waved.

She blew them a kiss, and headed off to work, the happiness in her heart today outweighing the uncertainty.

*

Drooms determined not to think of his new neighbor as he walked the six blocks to the subway station. There were more important things to think about, though he wished she had moved to a different floor, so as not to bother him. He hoped she and her boys would keep to themselves, the way the other tenants did.

Drooms resented the intrusions from other people, always trying to burden him with their emotions. The smiling chestnut vendor grated on him as much as the sour-faced street sweeper. The cheerful subway riders annoyed him even more than the grumpy ones. Though by far the worst were the people who took it upon themselves to speak to him, who attempted to engage him in conversation.

"Terrible news," they might say as they glanced up from their newspapers.

Or, "Getting colder," as they looked up at the sky.

Even a silent head shake or a simple smile felt like someone had just opened the door to his apartment and barged right in. What business was it of his what they all thought? His new neighbor could just keep to herself, he thought, tugging his hat lower on his brow.

*

Meanwhile, at the office of Charles Drooms Accounting, the stout office manager, Mrs. Murphy, clapped her hands when one of the staff accountants walked through the door carrying a pine garland.

"A wonderful idea, Mr. Finch! I was just thinking it was time to put up the holiday decorations."

Mrs. Murphy adjusted the brooch on the lapel of her tweed suit. Though Christmas was still weeks away, she had rummaged through her holiday jewelry this morning and decided to wear the little green wreath with the red bow and red rhinestone holly berries. The coincidence of her choosing to wear her Christmas brooch today and Finch bringing in the fresh pine bough made it the official beginning of the holiday season for her.

With the help of Finch, Mrs. Murphy lifted the old box of decorations from the top shelf of the coat closet and set it on her desk. Then she began directing the staff on where to hang the Christmas decorations.

"A gold garland and tinsel for you," she said, handing the items to the typist. "And you can help Mr. Finch with the pine bough," she said to one of the accountants.

As Finch tacked up the greenery around the doorframe, Mrs. Murphy put her hand to her chest and inhaled.

"Ah, the scent of Christmas. How lovely!"

She continued to hand out more items as the employees arrived: a few Santa hats, a set of tiny reindeer, boxes of ornaments, and a pinecone wreath.

The holiday activity and the scent of woodland pine energized them as they discussed their plans for the weekend, the morning offering the best opportunity for catching up.

By 8:30 there must be no lingering chitchat. They were on the clock after all, and Drooms expected them to be in full work mode by the time he arrived.

Mrs. Murphy hung a few glass ornaments on the gold garland that was now looped over the credenza. She stepped back to admire her work.

"Let's finish this up before himself arrives."

The typist held the box of tinsel and carefully pulled out long, shimmery strands and draped them on the pine branches around the door. She glanced at the clock.

"That gives us exactly ten and one half minutes."

"Less talk, more work!" barked Finch, as he donned a Santa hat and scowled.

The typist laughed at his antics and tossed a few strands of tinsel on his hat.

*

Though largely oblivious to the world around him, Drooms became increasingly annoyed as the signs of the Christmas season rudely imposed themselves upon him.

First, a shopkeeper and his wife blocked his way with a string of colored bulbs as they hung it from their store awning, forcing Drooms into an unwilling dance as he attempted to get around them.

Then, as he rounded a corner, he nearly tripped over a Christmas tree as a vendor arranged fresh-cut pines and firs along the sidewalk outside his store.

A final Christmas affront came outside the office building when a Salvation Army bell ringer, dressed as Santa, rang the bell in Drooms's ear just as he walked by.

When Drooms finally entered his office, the holiday merriment in his staff was too much for him. What were they thinking, lollygagging with Santa hats and garlands in their hands?

"Less talk, more work!" he snapped.

He ignored the ripple of low laughter and looked around for his senior accountant and right-hand man.

"Where's Mason?"

Mrs. Murphy recognized her boss's Christmas frame of mind and continued hanging the silver bells outside his office, causing them to jingle as she gave them a final tap.

"And a good morning to you, sir. I'm sure Mr. Mason will be in soon."

"Well, send him into my office when he arrives." Drooms looked fixedly at the clock, in justification of his bad temper, and then stepped into his office and closed the door.

The new clerk stood frozen, holding the other end of the gold garland while the typist finished scalloping it above their desks. Mrs. Murphy patted him on the shoulder and went back to the old box to dig out some red ribbon.

"Oh, carry on, carry on. He's all bark. I've been putting up these decorations for nigh on twenty years."

Through the glass door of his office, Drooms watched his staff put the final touches around their desks. He knew he had overreacted, but it was his habit to be offended by holidays, especially this one. He looked in disgust at the wreath, the garlands, and ornaments.

"Christmastime," he muttered as he sat at his desk. "Again!"

*

At an office building across town, Lillian stood in front of a large Christmas tree in the lobby. It sparkled with red garlands and bunches of tinsel, and from its branches dangled red and gold balls and silver snowflakes. A workman leaned in from atop a tall ladder and secured a large silver star at the top.

Izzy, Lillian's friend and co-worker, pushed through the revolving door and smiled when she saw Lillian gaping up at the tree like a child.

"Morning, Lilly!"

Lillian's face showed surprise. "Back today? I didn't expect you until Monday." She gave Izzy a quick hug.

"I wanted to spend some time with Red this weekend," Izzy said.

Lillian heard a few onlookers clap and turned to see that the tree's multicolored bulbs had been lit.

"Oh, look, Izzy. Christmastime! Already!"

"Beautiful! I love this time of year."

"Gee, I'm glad you're back. How was your trip? How's your sister?"

"We had a swell time. Shopping and luncheons, time with the kids – they had a Christmas play at school. So adorable. Makes me wish I had some of my own."

Lillian noticed Izzy's new deep green coat and took a step back to admire it.

"Oh, it's beautiful! Velvet collar and cuffs. Very smart."

"We spent a whole day shopping, mostly just looking. But I needed a new coat, and I couldn't resist the color: Twilight Forest, the saleslady called it."

Izzy recapped the highlights of her trip as they walked to the elevators. "Enough about me. How are things – are you feeling more settled in? How are the boys adjusting?"

"Oh fine, fine."

Izzy gave her a skeptical look. "C'mon, out with it. I know when you're bluffing."

Lillian lowered her voice. "Well, I'm not sure. Gabriel's been wetting the bed. He never has before."

Izzy waved away the concern. "It's just a phase. Perfectly natural."

"I suppose so. And Tommy's been acting up lately. It's not like him. You know, he didn't want to leave the old neighborhood."

"Well, you didn't have much choice, did you?"

"No. They say the whole street will be shops soon. But I didn't have the heart to tell him. He'll be so upset." They just missed one elevator and waited for another. "But I have a good feeling about the new place. I think the boys will be happy there."

"Of course they will. They just need time to adjust. And I think it's a good change for you. Time to get on with your life."

"Oh, not that again. I've got my life just the way I want it. I can't handle any more changes."

"What about that handsome man down the hall?"

Lillian turned in surprise. "Did I say that?"

Izzy smiled at the sudden blush in Lillian's cheeks. "No. But somehow I got that impression."

Lillian shook her head at Izzy's ongoing attempts at matchmaking. "He's not at all friendly. I was just hoping to have nice neighbors. That's all." Her decision to move had nothing to do with finding someone to replace Tom. The very thought filled her with repugnance. She was glad the crowded elevator prevented Izzy from continuing the conversation.

But as soon as they got off on their floor, Izzy started up again. "Well, someone else then."

"No, Izzy," said Lillian, as they headed down the hall to the main office of Rockwell Publishing. "Truly. I'm content with the way things are. All I care about is giving my boys a good home. I just hope they adjust."

"Don't worry, Lilly. It'll get better. You'll see. And Red has a couple of buddies in mind if you change your mind about double dating."

Lillian started to object, then realized that Izzy couldn't help herself, that she loved to see people paired off and happy.

They walked through the open glass doors into the large office that was already bustling with messengers running here and there, workers settling in for the day, phones ringing.

"It's way too early for *that*," Izzy said, pointing her chin across the room. The office manager, Mr. Weeble, a pinched birdlike man, peered over his spectacles at them and tapped his watch.

Izzy tossed him a sarcastic smile and pointed to her own watch. "We still have five minutes. God,

that lizard makes me sick. Are we on for lunch?"
she asked, taking her seat among the typists.

Lillian held up her sack lunch, and then
hurried into the switchboard room. Every day
she was thankful for the job Izzy had helped her
to get. Without office experience, it had been
difficult for her to find a position. After months
of being turned down, she finally accepted Izzy's
help and took the telephone operator job at the
publishing house as a way of getting her foot in
the door.

It was a huge improvement from the
department store position she had for the last
five years. At least she could sit at this job; years
of standing had taken a toll on her feet and
legs. Now, after just four months, the aches and
numbness were almost gone. She was saving for
a typewriter and hoped to work her way up to a
better position; but her deepest hope was to join
the Art Department. She was putting together
a portfolio, working on illustrations that leant
themselves to magazines. This job could be the
door to her long-buried dreams.

The only blot on her workday came from the
owner, Mr. Randolph Rockwell, recently divorced
from his high-society wife. Whenever Lillian
passed by him, he looked at her with a hungry, cov-
etous eye that completely unnerved her. She tried
to ignore him and trusted that her lowly status was

protection against any interest in her. She resented the talk of the office girls about playing her cards right and not acting so coy. With the exception of Izzy, she kept to herself and just tried to do a good job.

Lillian greeted the other two operators, and after hanging her coat and hat on the hook behind her chair, she settled into her station.

She took a small sketchbook from her bag, and began to answer the lights, drawing and doodling between calls. She made a quick sketch of Mr. Weeble as a lizard, and was pleased at the likeness.

Just then she felt a tap on her shoulder and turned to see him standing right behind her. He was not amused by the drawing.

Lillian, flustered, shut her sketchbook and stood. "Yes, Mr. Weeble?"

"You are not being paid for your artistic talents, Mrs. Hapsey."

"No. Of course not."

He motioned to the other operators to pay attention to the incoming calls.

Lillian felt herself grow warm and regretted her folly. "Is there anything else, Mr. Weeble?"

"Indeed, there is." He coughed and brushed some lint from his sleeve, prolonging her anxiety.

"Mr. Rockwell wishes to see you."

"Mr. Rockwell? Wishes to see me?"

"I believe I spoke clearly." He pursed his mouth, pivoted, and walked away, leaving Lillian to trail behind him. As they crossed the busy floor, he glanced down at his heels occasionally, making Lillian feel like she was a small pet who must follow.

At the president's office, Mr. Weeble nodded to Mr. Rockwell's secretary, gave a parting look at Lillian over his spectacles, and went to the large oak desk situated on a platform where he could oversee the staff.

Mr. Rockwell's secretary, a woman in a tight-fitting sweater and bright red lips, winked at Lillian before announcing her.

"Good luck, kid," she whispered, and then closed the door once Lillian was inside.

When Lillian saw that Mr. Rockwell was on the phone she started to leave, but he motioned for her to sit down. Lillian sank into the deep wing-back chair, but it fit her all wrong. She scooted to the edge and placed her hands in her lap. With sidelong glances she took in the beauty of Mr. Rockwell's suite – the Persian rug, the gleaming wood paneling, the spectacular view of the city.

He finished the call and stood.

Lillian quickly stood as well. "Good morning, Mr. Rockwell." She blushed to find herself alone with the owner of the publishing house.

Mr. Rockwell dipped his head to the side, but didn't smile. Lillian knew that most people would consider him handsome, but she found him unattractive and disliked the way he was always evaluating women's figures. She folded her arms, putting one hand to her neck.

Rockwell walked around his large mahogany desk and took her hand, holding it longer than was necessary. He then leaned against his desk and waited a few seconds before speaking.

"Mrs. Haspey. I trust you are well."

Lillian smiled faintly and blinked at the floor.

"Please. Sit."

Again she felt like a small pet. She sat on the edge of the chair, her brow lightly furrowed.

Rockwell frowned at her uneasiness. "No need to look so uncomfortable. I just wanted to ask you: Do you like the theater?"

Lillian had been focusing on the back of the desk, but she now looked up as if she had perhaps misunderstood him.

"The theater?"

He appeared slightly put out that his overture wasn't met with more enthusiasm.

"I have box tickets to a performance next Saturday. I was wondering if you would like to accompany me?"

"Oh. Thank you, Mr. Rockwell. Thank you, but I can't. My son hasn't been feeling well lately. I need to be home with him."

Rockwell didn't believe her for a moment, but accepted her refusal. A hard-to-get woman always whetted his appetite more than the pliable type. He gave a low, almost inaudible chuckle, as if he were onto her game.

"Well. Another time, then."

Lillian stood up and pressed her lips together in a thwarted smile.

His eyes traveled over her legs, and then her dress, before resting on her face. "Good day." He held the door open for her.

Lillian murmured "Good day," and quickly left his office, relieved to hear the door close behind her. She put a cool hand to her warm cheek, but then caught the unexpected scent of his cologne on her hand.

She went to the ladies room, turned on the faucet, and rolled the bar of soap around and around, until the smell was gone. She then splashed cold water on her face, and as she patted her face dry, she saw her pretty blue dress in the mirror and regretted that she had worn it. She would return it to the back of her closet. Tomorrow she would wear her gray suit.

*

Drooms noted the time when Mason arrived. Fifteen minutes late. Drooms waved him in, and waited impatiently while Mason hurriedly hung up his coat and hat. They briefly discussed a letter that Mason needed to draft regarding a particular account.

Mason then settled into his desk, shuffled through some folders, and soon became absorbed in his work. He had a way of smoothing down his dark moustache when deeply considering something, and Drooms noticed him doing this repeatedly through-out the morning. He assumed Mason was simply disconcerted at being late, and gave it no more thought.

Drooms later invited him to lunch, as he often did. There was a particular subject he wanted to broach, gauge Mason's response. Drooms valued Mason's steady, solid business sense; he was open-minded, far-seeing, and flexible, up to a point – he would bend so far, and then no more, and nothing could change his mind. And Drooms had never known him to be wrong. Drooms was usually sure of his business moves, but this one had him doubting himself to some degree.

As they walked down the busy street to their usual restaurant, an attractive woman in a sleek black coat and fashionable little boots stopped on recognizing Drooms. She placed her hand on his arm.

"Why hello, Charles!"

Drooms furrowed his brow in annoyance as he tried to place the face, then softened somewhat.

"Oh. Hello." He took his arm back to lightly tip his hat. "Mason, you remember Miss Bentley?"

The ever-cordial Mason smiled warmly. "Of course. So nice to see you again. How have you been?" He remembered Miss Bentley as a pleasant woman Drooms had dated a few years ago. Mason had hoped it might develop into a serious relationship, perhaps even marriage. But he had seen this pattern in Drooms for years, and was not surprised when he unexpectedly broke it off. Mason was rather amazed that Miss Bentley seemed so pleased to see Drooms.

For his part, Drooms hoped Mason wasn't going to start with his pleasantries as he tended to do. It was too cold to be chatting in the middle of a crowded sidewalk. Drooms cast a worried glance at the sky, as if it might suddenly open up with rain or snow, and that they needed to get a move on.

"I've been very well, thank you, Mr. Mason." Miss Bentley had a stylish, confident air about her, yet there was also an asking, perhaps a neediness, that came through her manner. She faced Drooms, and once again lightly placed her gloved hand on his sleeve.

"Goodness, it's been ages. How are you?"

That touch of familiarity was all it took for Drooms to firmly shut any door that she might think was still open. He believed that when things were finished, they were finished. No need to get things started up again. He looked at his watch, preventing any chance of conversation. "I'm fine, thank you. I'm sorry, but we have a business engagement we can't be late for."

Her lips parted in surprise at his brusqueness, then pursed in remembrance. She pulled her coat closer around her.

"The same as ever, I see. Goodbye, Mr. Drooms!" To Mason she spoke more gently. "Goodbye." She then left, shaking her head.

Drooms and Mason walked a few steps in silence, then Mason spoke out. "I rather liked Miss Bentley. Thought she would be good for you."

"You know my motto, Mason."

Mason had often heard this from Drooms.

"No attachments."

"That's right," said Drooms. "They just get in the way."

They entered the restaurant with its dark paneling, polished wood floors, and deep green leather upholstery, and made their way through the tables of businessmen. White-clad waiters moved briskly among the tables. The clinking of glasses and of utensils against china mixed with the hum of conversation. A fine haze of cigar and cigarette smoke hung in the air.

Mason studied the menu while Drooms continued his train of thought with a detached smile, as if thinking of something pleasant.

"No attachments. Which brings me to the purpose of this meeting. I'm going to acquire Henderson's."

Mason's head popped up. "You mean merge? Henderson agrees to this?"

Drooms leaned forward, staring intently. "I'm talking takeover, Mason."

Mason slowly sat back, shaking his head and stroking his moustache. "After all these years. I consider Howard a friend. We can't just –"

"This is business. Not a picnic."

With a quick flick, Drooms shook out his napkin and placed it on his lap. He was annoyed that Mason met the discussion with immediate disapproval. Always on his high horse about everything. Drooms opened the menu, and then closed it, remembering his strongest argument.

"Are you forgetting what happened when you started with me? Are you forgetting the lawsuit?"

Mason's mouth dropped open. "But that was his father – and he's been dead for ten years!"

Drooms perused the menu, unperturbed by Mason's reaction. "Business is business."

"It sounds more like revenge," said Mason.

Drooms chuckled lightly at this notion. "Revenge? You're too sentimental, Mason. I told you – it's business." He snapped the menu shut, and called the waiter.

Chapter 2

All day Drooms felt distracted, irritable. As he rode the subway home, he tried to trace the source of his distraction – had it started with Mason's disapproval of the takeover? Or was it the morning's Christmas nonsense in the office? Or had it begun even earlier, with his intrusive new neighbor calling out to him? No matter. The day was nearly over now.

Some murky inner prompting caused Drooms to suddenly decide to get off one station early, bumping the passengers in his rush to get out before the train doors closed. He hurried out of the station, thinking that he would stop by The Red String Curio Store. That would calm his mind.

The Red String was one of the few stores Drooms looked at now and then. Though he took great pleasure in his work and allowed it to take over most of his waking hours, he did have one interest outside of work, a sort of hobby, though he kept it to himself.

He opened the door to The Red String Curio Store, its little bell ringing as he entered. That silvery sound was the first signal that he was leaving behind him the outer workaday world; the musty old attic smell was the second, a scent only slightly masked by the baskets of orange peel and cloves set among the shelves.

The store owner, a bald little man wearing a red bowtie and high-waisted trousers held up with red suspenders, his style since the turn of the century, stood at the counter helping an elderly lady to choose between two old birdcages. He held up a finger as a greeting to Drooms.

The front of the store was full with displays of new toys and gifts for the holiday. But for the most part, the store was a dusty jumble of shelves and aisles crowded with old furniture, used books and magazines, cracked and mismatched dishes alongside near-complete sets, lamps and lanterns, boxes of odds and ends.

The walls themselves could barely be seen, covered as they were by mirrors of all shapes and sizes, still-lifes and landscapes of various quality, and empty frames. A few sagging tapestries depicted once-vibrant stag hunts and pastoral courtships; their subjects had long since been lulled by time and now appeared too tired for action of any kind.

On the back wall, hung worn posters advertising everything from travel to exotic Egypt and the Levant, to performances of *The Pirates of Penzance* and *Carmen*, to soap – a Palmolive-scented mother poised above her sleeping child; an elegant 1920's couple dancing on their toes, almost floating above the words *Erasmic Soaps & Perfumes*.

Scattered throughout the store were wall clocks and grandfather clocks set to different times, so that ticking and deep resonant chimes filled the air at all hours, punctuated now and then by an occasional cuckoo.

Drooms wandered through the front aisles, his eyes leisurely scanning the shelves and counters and cases, the worn wooden floor creaking under his step. He almost tripped over a young man sitting in one of the faded overstuffed chairs, sorting through a box of old daguerreotypes and postcards.

Along the wall, Drooms passed glass cabinets filled with buttons and shoe hooks, pocket watches and Victorian jewelry, musical instruments and sheet music, and items of unrecognizable use. An old man in a long, thread-bare coat leaned against a glass case and plucked the out-of-tune strings of a dusty violin, humming along as he did so.

At the end of the glass cabinets, Drooms turned down the maze-like aisles with shelves that reached past his shoulders. His mind always moved more freely in the timeless hodgepodge of the store, the worries and distractions of the day diminished as he searched out an item, or stumbled upon an unexpected find. He sometimes found that several hours had passed while he wandered among the aisles.

But today his mind was focused. He felt the need to add to his collection. He moved to the far back of the shop where he often found what he was looking for, and after browsing for a short while, he lifted an item from a low shelf and inspected it.

A few minutes later, the little bell rang as he left the store carrying a parcel tied in red string.

He was often seen coming home with such a package and his neighbors had long since given up wondering what it was that Old Man Drooms collected. They were sure the boxes and bundles were not gifts; his were not the kind of packages that brought happiness, or caused the giver to take two steps at a time in eagerness to give them. Rather, the parcels seemed a kind of burden to him. If anything, Drooms's step was heavier as he walked home.

At the corner of his block, Drooms stopped by the neighborhood grocery store to pick up a few items for the weekend. The owners, Mr. and Mrs. Mancetti, were busy at the counter but they lifted their heads in greeting and noticed the package under his arm. Drooms gave an almost imperceptible tip of his hat, and lifted a store hand basket.

He chose a loaf of bread, some fresh ground coffee, a bottle of milk. Not caring much about what he ate, he tended to buy the same things over and over. He reached for a few cans of soup and a box of crackers, a tin of peaches and a box of noodles, and placed them in the basket.

When Drooms approached the front counter, he realized that the owner had been gossiping about him to the two customers near the door, for they stood smiling, as if in anticipation of some fun. One of them jerked his head to Mancetti, coaxing him to go ahead and say something.

"Evening, Mr. Drooms," said Mancetti.

Drooms took his things from the basket and set them on the counter.

"So," said Mancetti, as he began to ring up the items, "I understand the beautiful widow Hapsey has moved down the hall from you."

"That's no concern of mine." Drooms set the tin of peaches firmly on the counter. "Or yours," he added.

"No, no, of course not. Just making small talk." He finished ringing up Drooms, and Mrs. Mancetti handed Drooms his bag of items, smiling kindly.

Drooms nodded goodnight to her, but ignored her smirking husband and the other two customers.

*

The sky delivered on its promise of snow and by end of day a light accumulation covered the sidewalks. The temperature had dropped, turning some of the heavily trodden snow to ice.

Lillian made her way home with care, trying to avoid the slick spots on the sidewalks, and wishing she had worn her boots. Her thoughts were on fixing dinner for Tommy and Gabriel, but as she rounded the corner to her block, she was struck by the beauty of the street. She had never seen it in the snow.

She stopped and let her gaze linger up and down the street, taking it all in. The tree branches were delicately outlined in snow, as were the railings and balustrades of the brownstones. Dusk was deepening, and from the streetlights hung soft golden curtains of falling snow. She looked at the fading sky and wondered which paints she would mix for that shade, how to capture the nuances of that deepening blue-gray.

She caught the scent of wood fire from one of the chimneys, and deeply inhaled the clear cold air, thinking that it smelled of snow and softness and dusk.

Further down the street, some of the neighborhood children were out reveling in the first snowfall, laughing and shouting. Warm yellow light poured forth from the windows, holding the promise of the comforts of home.

Lillian's heart was lifted, grateful to be a part of such ordinary loveliness. Sometimes she was flooded with such a feeling, almost like euphoria, but tinged with sadness because it was so fleeting. She had long thought of these moments as the edge of desire – a desperate longing for something beyond her grasp, just at the periphery of knowing. Yet ever elusive. While it lasted, she felt as though she had stepped into some heightened state, absolutely connected to life.

Just then, Mrs. Wilson, who lived in the same apartment building as the babysitter, called out from behind, pulling Lillian back down to the solidity of the sidewalk beneath her feet, the coldness of her fingers, the need to start dinner.

"Evening, Mrs. Hapsey. You must be frozen just standing there. What *you* need is a good head scarf, far more practical for keeping out the wind and cold." She tightened her brown plaid scarf, and with a flick of her hand, gestured to some imaginary group behind her. "Let the other women wear their *fashionable* hats."

"Good evening, Mrs. Wilson."

Mrs. Wilson took Lillian's arm. "I was hoping to make it home before the snow and ice began. How're you faring?"

"Fine. Just on my way to pick up the boys."

They continued down the sidewalk together, careful of their step.

"I heard that Mrs. Kuntzman is babysitting them."

"The boys love her," said Lillian.

"She's a godsend. You know, she used to watch my kids. That was long years ago." Mrs. Wilson's tone slid into friendly sarcasm. "And how do you get on with that neighbor of yours down the hall?"

"Oh, you mean Mr. Drooms? Well – he's not very talkative."

"Talkative? He's a perfect curmudgeon. Won't give me the time of day. Or anyone."

Drooms had just rounded the corner and was walking towards them.

"Speak of the devil. There he is. With one of his *packages*."

Lillian saw Drooms approaching, holding a parcel under one arm and a bag of groceries in the other. She smiled as the large snowflakes fell on her upturned face, blinking as they caught on her eyelashes.

"Good evening, Mr. Drooms," she said. "Look! Our first snowfall. Isn't it lovely?"

Drooms stopped and looked around, as if noticing the snow for the first time. "So it is."

But as he glanced up he slipped on the snow, lost his balance, and grabbed at the railing, which caused him to drop his package.

Lillian instinctively reached out to help him but also slipped on the same patch and had to steady herself on the railing. She laughed as she picked up his package and handed it to him. "I see you've begun your Christmas shopping."

Drooms snatched the package from her, scowled, and continued down the sidewalk.

Lillian's hand went to her cheek, her hat, taken aback by his abrupt, unexpected response. "Goodness! He is a bit cranky."

Mrs. Wilson gave a snort as if to say, I told you so. They walked up the brownstone steps and heard a knock at Mrs. Kuntzman's window. Mrs. Wilson waved at Tommy and Gabriel. "There they are. How old?"

"Nine and six," Lillian said. The boys shouted something through the window, pointing to the papers in their hands.

"My, but they're cute. They remind me of mine when they were that age. Of course, back then I didn't have to worry myself about Mrs. Kuntzman's German accent. Everyone's suspicious now, with Herr Hitler on the rampage. And now with this so-called *peacetime* conscription of ours."

"Perhaps it won't come to that." Lillian so dreaded the thought of war.

"You don't build up an army unless you plan to use it," said Mrs. Wilson. "Mark my words."

They opened the door and stomped the snow off their shoes in the vestibule. Mrs. Wilson untied her scarf and shook out the wet snow. "Well, gotta run and get dinner started for Harry. I'll see you around!"

"So long!" Lillian had a sick feeling in her stomach about war developing and feared it was just a matter of time. But she hoped that people weren't treating Mrs. Kuntzman unkindly. People didn't come any better than her, whatever her accent.

*

Drooms, meanwhile, arrived home. He checked his mailbox and took out a lone envelope. Postmarked Illinois. A Christmas card. He held it a moment, and then tossed it into the grocery bag.

He trudged up the stairs to the third floor, and opened the door to his apartment, still disconcerted by his clumsiness on the sidewalk. He never stumbled. Then just as he had that thought, he tripped on the threshold and dropped his keys. As he bent to pick them up, he glowered at Lillian's apartment. "The last thing I need is an intrusive neighbor – with noisy kids!" He opened his door, went inside, and slammed the door behind him.

*

Lillian smiled as Mrs. Kuntzman opened her door. The babysitter was wearing one of her flowered aprons and was cheerful as usual.

Gabriel and Tommy ran to the door, holding up paper snowflakes.

"Look, Mommy!" said Gabriel. "Mrs. Kuntzman showed us how to make snowflakes!"

"Look! Mrs. Kuntzman says to string them and hang them," added Tommy.

Lillian opened her eyes wide and bent over to admire the boys' artwork. "Oh, how wonderful!" She turned the paper snowflakes over in her hands. "Now we have something for our windows." She beamed at Mrs. Kuntzman, appreciative of her never-ending efforts with the boys. "Go get your coats on. I'll hold your snowflakes."

Lillian looked closely at Mrs. Kuntzman, thinking that she must still have family in Germany. She must feel torn. Anyone would. "Any problems today?"

"Ach, no! We had a fine time. Such good boys. They even finish their homework."

"Already?"

"And," said Mrs. Kuntzman, holding up a finger — she went to the kitchen and returned with a plate covered with a red and white checked napkin — "I have extra strudel for youse. Still warm. I always make too much."

Lillian recognized Mrs. Kuntzman's modest way of being generous, and graciously accepted the plate. "Thank you." She lifted the cloth and inhaled. "It smells delicious! We'll have it for dessert tonight." She made a mental note to add some ingredients for baking when she returned the plate. Some raisins and nuts, perhaps, or better yet, some cherry preserves.

The boys were already at the door, fastening their boots and buttoning their coats. "Bye, Mrs. Kuntzman!" they hollered, eager to get out in the snow.

"We'll see you on Monday," said Lillian.

"Goodnight, Mrs. Hapsey. See youse all next week!"

Once they were outside, the boys saw the neighborhood kids playing in the snow.

"Can we play outside?" Tommy asked. "Mickey and Billy are there."

"Can we, Mommy? Please?" asked Gabriel.

Lillian saw the growing number of children playing in the falling snow. "Well, for a few minutes, while I get dinner ready. Put your hats and gloves on. And stay on the sidewalk where I can see you. And don't cross the street. Okay, Tommy? You'll watch your brother?"

Tommy rolled his eyes. "I always do, Mom. You don't have to tell me every single time."

"I know." She reached out to him but he dodged her and hurried off with Gabriel. She hoped the undercurrent of anger in him, at having to leave all his old friends, would lessen as he made new ones. She took it as a good sign that he was eager to play with the kids.

When Lillian entered her apartment, she stepped out of her shoes, hung her coat and hat on the hall tree, and turned on the lamps, breathing a deep sigh of pleasure to be back in her haven. She looked around, thinking that the apartment had turned out well.

She had used every spare minute of the last three weeks unpacking and trying to recreate the feel of home. The layout was a little different from their old place. The living room and kitchen were divided by a chest-high half wall, which gave the feel of one large open room.

It was a cozy place – small, but big enough for them. New, yet familiar too, with things from their old home: the burgundy velvet couch and arm-chairs with the embroidered pillows her mother had made; the pale green Fiestaware vase from her sister, Annette; the carved mirror that the fellows from the firehouse had given as a wedding present.

She smiled as she remembered the card: "From our House to Yours: To reflect Lillian's beauty and Tom's vanity." Tom hadn't been at all vain, but he did have a cowlick that never stayed down that the guys used to tease him about.

And above the fireplace, Millet's *The Angelus* that she had loved as a child, with its sunset mackerel sky, its furrowed field, the distant village – the painting that had first inspired her to want to draw, to mix colors, to capture the sky. A parting gift from her parents when she had joined Tom in New York City.

How she missed her parents. Her childhood and youth in Rhinebeck, upstate, were full of happy memories of her parents and sister. Times had been lean, but their lives had always been full of daily riches: her mother's beautifully set table and wonderful meals, lamplit evenings on the porch, long walks when the weather was fine.

Lillian had been especially close to her mother and enjoyed many of the same pleasures. It was her mother who had encouraged her to read, and draw, to study history and literature. Annette had been more like her father – taking pleasure in running the drygoods store, and helping him with the large vegetable garden. But they had all been close. It was a real blow when first her mother, and then her father, died, just before Gabriel was born. Her parents had always been a romantic, inseparable couple, and could not live one without the other.

Lillian turned on the radio and adjusted the knob to find a music station. She went to the kitchen window and looked down at the street. There was Tommy with his new best friend, Mickey, leading some kind of game, with Gabriel and the younger kids running first in one direction, then in another.

She hummed along with the radio as she moved about the kitchen preparing dinner, thinking that the fresh bread she picked up on her way home would go nicely with yesterday's stew. When a swing band began to play "In the Mood," she turned up the volume and took a few steps with an imaginary partner. She and Tom had spent many evenings in their early days twirling and stepping to the new rhythms.

She lifted the lid to the stew and inhaled, and then sliced the bread, and began to set the table. It was a simple meal, but the boys never complained. Still, she was glad for Mrs. Kuntzman's strudel.

When the radio began to play "I'll Never Smile Again," she started to sing along. But then she abruptly stopped, and with the soup bowls still in her hands, she sat down at the table and stared out at nothing.

Sometimes all it took was a strain of melody to remind her of how alone she really was. When the boys were around, she didn't have time to think about it.

Lillian leaned back in the chair and lightly shook her head, thinking how long ago it seemed that she and Tom had been young and in love. Sometimes she felt that they had never really had the chance to get to know each other, to grow together as adults, the way her parents had. She had gotten pregnant immediately, and when Tom lost his job, she had moved back home while he looked for work in the city. Six brief years together, and then his unexpected death.

When she thought of Tom, it was as the young, boyish man she had married. So much had changed. She had changed. After his death, she had to shake off her girlhood and take on the responsibilities of both mother and father.

She rose quickly and finished setting the table. She had done away with the "if only" habit that left her feeling empty and forlorn: if only Tom had not rushed into the burning building, if only her parents had lived and she could have gone back home.

Tom was gone, and her life was here now. Over the years she had come to love the city, and the fellows at the firehouse and their wives still treated her like family and invited her to gatherings.

And she had her beloved sister, though she only saw her once or twice a year. Annette had stayed with her during those first terrible months, and had even considered making Brooklyn her home. But she had gone back to marry her childhood sweetheart, and was at her happiest helping him run the orchard. She kept Lillian and the boys well supplied in apple butter, bottled pears, and cherry and apricot preserves. And she now had three little ones of her own. At least Lillian always had that haven to return to in the summers.

Lillian shut off the radio and looked out the window again at her boys. She almost raised the sash to call them inside, but decided she would go out instead. Dinner was ready and the boys had finished their homework. She could afford a few moments of play with them. That's what Tom would have done, she thought. She shut off the stove, and put on her boots and coat.

*

When Drooms arrived home, he placed his bags on the kitchen counter, and went to the living room to put the Christmas card in the top desk drawer, along with the others from previous years. To be opened later, perhaps in the spring.

He went back to the kitchen and put away the groceries. He then fixed himself a sandwich, poured a glass of milk, and ate his dinner at the kitchen counter as he listened to the radio. Now and then he thumbed through the stacks of files on the kitchen table, which was used as a work space. When the news came on, he shook his head.

"Nothing but trouble. Trouble everywhere."

It seemed like just yesterday he was positioned off Ireland, and later in the North Sea. The war to end war, indeed. Now here they were, at it again. He supposed he was too old to serve again, but if called upon, of course he would go. He didn't like what he was hearing from Europe. He brushed the crumbs from his hands and turned off the radio.

The package from The Red String Curio Store sat on the kitchen counter, still in its brown

paper and red string. Drooms prolonged the opening of it, saving it to give shape to his evening, a
little break before starting on the paperwork he
always concluded the day with. He finished his
sandwich, washed his plate, and set it in the dish
rack. Only then did he take the package into the
living room.

Drooms set the parcel on the large oak desk
and untied the string, speaking aloud as he did so,
speaking in a kinder tone than he had used all day.

"Now. Let's take a look at you. See how you
fit in with the others."

He slid off the red string, unwrapped the
brown paper, and pulled out a stuffed squirrel. He
set it on his desk, took a step back, and assessed it.

"Not bad. Not bad."

He walked to the tall bookcase that held several other taxidermic animals – stiff little things
with glittering eyes and sharp claws, arranged in
action, so to speak: stuffed birds preened in their
nests, small animals clung to branches, the larger
owl and fox stalked from the top of the case. For
the most part, the shelves were full of animals that
nested or perched or stood ready for attack, in frozen animation.

One by one, over the years, the animals had
taken over the bookcase, squeezing out the history
books and novels, the atlases and reference books.
Russian novels and Roman history, in particular,

had held Drooms's attention as a young man. But his interest in those had dwindled at the same rate that his business had increased.

Only the bottom shelf was still piled high with books, and a few thick tomes were positioned here and there on the shelves, to provide elevation for the smaller animals, or a better vantage point, in the case of the sparrow hawk. The rest of the books had long ago been boxed and stored in the room between his bedroom and living room, a sort of large closet where things from the past were packed away and forgotten.

However, even when his schedule was the fullest and business was at its most demanding, Drooms still made time for the animals. Most of the pieces came from the scattered remnants of naturalists' collections from the previous century, or were old trophies from hunters long gone.

Drooms stood back now and admired the collection he had amassed. There they were – poised in perfection. Self-sufficient little things. He never had to worry about them; no harm could come to them now.

"Make room," he spoke to them all. "We have an addition. Another squirrel." He moved aside a red squirrel. "Don't worry, this one is a gray."

He placed the new squirrel near a mossy branch, stood back and tilted his head from one side, then to the other. Satisfied, he nodded.

"Yes. Very life-like."

He picked up a small, stuffed brown rabbit and absent-mindedly caressed it.

"Well, what do you think? Hmm? You're the expert."

Just then he heard voices and laughter coming from the street below. He walked to the living room window, then backed up slightly so as not to be seen. The widow Hapsey was down there with her two sons, laughing and catching snowflakes with them. He couldn't help but notice how attractive she was. Beautiful, really – so full of life. Not that it mattered. He watched her until she gathered up her boys and went inside.

Drooms continued to gaze out the window, remembering a snowy afternoon from long ago, this same time of year: his mother, smiling in the doorway, calling him and his siblings in to dinner. Snow falling, the scent of her cooking wafting outside, the twins racing to the door. Those wonderful winter evenings on the farm. Nothing had ever really compared to them.

As the night darkened, Drooms's vision shifted from the soft-edged images of long ago to the sharpness of his angular reflection staring back at him in the window. He briefly looked into his shadowy eyes, and then with a brusque pull he closed the curtain – shutting out the night, the widow, and his memories.

Chapter 3

The snow fell softly all through the night, muffling sounds from the street and deepening sleep. It swirled around the window panes and drifted along the steps and balustrades of the brownstones.

By late morning, it was nearly a foot deep and still falling. Tommy and Gabriel had gone out early to play in the snow and had to be coaxed back inside for lunch. Now, a few hours later, Lillian and her boys emerged from the brownstone, all bundled up, on their way to the library.

The smooth drifts and untrammeled snow of early morning now showed signs of children at play. The pure peaked snow on the railings was ribbed by gloved fingers, the sidewalks were patterned with footprints and long lines from sled runners.

It seemed that all the neighborhood boys and girls were outside playing, thrilled that it was Saturday. There were a few attempts at snowmen and snow angels along the sidewalks. Across the street some of the older boys were having a snowball fight. Their laughter and shouting, whoops and cries filled the air. Their heads popped up between the parked cars as they dodged, and then threw, snowballs. Other kids darted behind trees or took shelter behind snowy barricades. Flashes of brightly striped stocking hats and colorful scarves enlivened the wintry day as the children crisscrossed from one side to the other, free from the worry of traffic. Today the street was all theirs.

Lillian held Gabriel's hand as they went down the steps, her other hand poised to reach for the balustrade should she slip.

"I don't want to go," Gabriel cried out in excitement. "I want to play outside again."

"When we get back," Lillian said. "We're going to need our books if it continues to snow."

Tommy spotted Mickey from next door and ran over to him. Then Gabriel broke free from Lillian's hand and ran over to Billy, one of Mickey's little brothers, to check on the snowman he was making.

Lillian looked in exasperation from one boy to the other. "Tommy! Gabriel! You can play when we get back."

She saw Mr. Drooms walking towards her and noticed that he was carrying his briefcase.

"Oh, Mr. Drooms, you didn't have to work today, did you – on Saturday?" She dodged a sled being pulled by some older kids.

Drooms instinctively took her elbow in protection as she stepped back, then quickly released it. "Just the morning."

Lillian couldn't help but compare that tiny, chivalrous gesture with Rockwell's presumptuous taking of her hand the other day. The arrogance behind that gesture still made her bristle. Drooms was definitely another kind of man, whatever his faults.

Tommy begrudgingly came back. Gabriel ran up to Drooms and pointed to the snowman. It had a hunched over appearance and a coal mouth that turned down.

"Hey, look, Mr. Drooms. Billy made a snowman of you!"

Lillian tried to brush away his comment.

"Gabriel, snowmen don't look like people –"

"Nuh uh, Billy said it was Old Man Drooms, that's Mr. –"

"Oh, hush!" She took Gabriel's hand and turned to Drooms. "We're off to the library."

"To get pirate books," said Tommy. "I can tell you about any pirate. Just ask me."

"Yeah, me too," said Gabriel. "Just ask me."

Tommy scoffed. "You can't read."

"I can too. Right, Mommy? I know how to read, Mr. Drooms."

"Picture books," Tommy said, under his breath.

Drooms looked down at Gabriel and spoke in a gentle tone that surprised Lillian. "Well, we all have to start at the beginning."

Gabriel smiled up at him.

As Drooms started to climb the steps, Lillian called out to him. "Can we pick up anything for you, Mr. Drooms?"

"No. Thank you," he said without turning around.

Tommy and Gabriel took Lillian by the hands and rushed her along in the snow. "C'mon, Mom!" She laughed with them as they made their way down the sidewalk.

Drooms stopped on the steps to look back at them, again noticing how attractive she was. She moved with a light gracefulness, the contours of her coat not quite concealing her pretty curves. Her glossy brown curls caught the sunlight as they brushed against the deep blue of her collar. The two boys ran ahead of her, urging her on. She put one hand on her hat and called out for them to slow down.

As Drooms watched them, the slightest of smiles began to form on his lips.

Then, out of nowhere – whack! He was smacked in the back of his head by a snowball.

He whipped around, scowling as he searched for the culprit. He caught a glimpse of an impish boy, around twelve or so, in a red scarf, laughing and ducking behind a car across the street.

Drooms took a few steps down and scanned the street, but the rascal seemed to have vanished. Drooms was disturbed, even angered, by this. He stood a few moments, narrowing his eyes as if remembering something. Then he shook his head and went inside.

He climbed the steps to his apartment, his briefcase suddenly growing heavy. He tried to shake away the feeling of unease. Work. That always cleared his head.

He made himself a strong cup of coffee and took it into the living room. He placed it on the large desk that dominated the room, opposite the couch and chair that he seldom used any more. The couch used to be his preferred place to read, with the lamp casting a soft light from behind.

Though Drooms was largely indifferent to his surroundings, he had, many years ago, indulged in a few paintings. His favorite was the large landscape, a harvest scene at sunset. Though it had hung over the couch for years, he had stopped seeing it.

He stood in front of it now, studying the partially cut field with sheaves of golden wheat; the dirt road deep with ruts, curving into an old farm; the leaves of the trees lining the road all reds and russet; a hazy orange sun sinking into the far-off hills. A few birds, crows he guessed, lifted from the field in the distance. The farmhouse windows shone with the yellow light of lamps, or perhaps they were reflecting the setting sun –

Drooms turned away impatiently, and settled into his desk. He didn't have time for sunsets and idle thoughts. His work demanded all his time.

He sipped his coffee and it was almost with pleasure that he became immersed in his ledgers and accounts. Still, from time to time a nagging feeling caused him to look out the window at the children playing, but he didn't see the boy in the red scarf. He finally dismissed it and continued with his work.

*

Just as the streetlights were coming on, Lillian and her boys returned from the library. Lillian was looking forward to losing herself in the novels she had chosen. A hot bath and some time in the English countryside, after she put the boys to bed, was her idea of a delightful weekend.

As they climbed to the third flor, Tommy and Gabriel talked about their books.

"Look, Gabe. This one is like the story on the radio – a ghost story."

"Well, don't read it at bedtime," said Lillian.

Tommy rolled his eyes and groaned, dragging his feet in exaggerated disbelief.

"Come on, boys, inside. How about we light a fire tonight? Won't that be cozy? I'll make dinner and then we can read by the fire."

*

Drooms heard Lillian and her boys arrive home and winced at all the noise they made chattering and stomping snow off their boots. He listened to their door close, vaguely wondering what kind of books she had chosen. He imagined her reading at her kitchen table with a cup of tea, or stretched out on the couch – or would she read in bed?

He sat up in his chair and cleared his throat, restacked the papers he was working on. His mind was all over the place today. He couldn't account for it. Not like him. He doubled the effort to focus on his work.

After a few hours, he realized that he was hungry and he took a break for dinner, making a quick meal of soup and toast. He then re-immersed himself in the ledgers. The numbers were better than he had expected. This was good. Very good. At this rate –

He heard a light knock at his door. He cocked his head to listen, but didn't hear anything more. Then he paused for a moment as he tried to remember if anyone had actually ever knocked at his door. Now that he thought of it, it seemed odd. He went back to his numbers.

But a few moments later, he again heard a soft knock. He put down his glasses and pencil, went to the door, and opened it.

Before him stood the same imp of a boy from the street, the one who threw the snowball, smiling with his tongue in his cheek, as if he knew he shouldn't be there. He twisted his red scarf and looked up, waiting for Drooms to make the next move.

Drooms stood frozen. At first he was simply shocked. Then he flushed in anger and slammed the door. He held his head in his hands and looked back up at the closed door. He quickly opened it – but there was no one there.

No one, except for Lillian. She stood in her doorway down the hall, wondering at the loud slam that shook her door, just as she was getting into her novel. She pulled her chenille robe close, holding the book in her hand.

"Is everything all right, Mr. Drooms?"

He was startled to see her but quickly recovered his composure.

"Yes. The wind just caught my door."

Lillian nodded at the explanation, and Drooms shut his door.

Lillian closed her door, and then realized the absurdity of the explanation. There was no wind. She started to reopen her door, but decided against it.

She made herself comfortable again on the couch, and gazed at the embers in the fireplace. The book lay face down on her lap. Something about him tugged at her. A kind of sadness, underneath the hardness, that she found difficult to ignore. She didn't entirely believe in his crusty exterior. The same way he probably didn't buy her ever-cheerful act, she guessed. The wounded always recognized each other.

A wry smile formed on her lips as she thought of what she had seen that morning. She had looked out the window to check on the boys, and saw Gabriel alone, trying his hardest to make a snowman, but the ball of snow kept crumbling. Then she saw Mr. Drooms walk down the steps, look around, and set his briefcase in the snow. That alone surprised her, but then he carefully packed a ball, showing Gabriel how to do it, and then began to roll it, shaping it as it grew. Then Gabriel rolled the ball and shrieked in delight as it grew rounder and fatter. She couldn't believe it. When a neighbor approached, Mr. Drooms picked up his briefcase, gave one of his curt nods, and continued on his way. His façade was full of all sorts of cracks and gaps.

She heard Gabriel scream and all thoughts of her neighbor vanished. She hurried to the boys' room and found Tommy laughing at Gabriel, who was peeking out from under his pillow.

Tommy held up an illustration in his pirate book. "Don't be so silly. It's just a story."

Lillian snatched the book from Tommy and looked at the picture of a skeleton pirate holding a sword to the throat of a frightened boy. The pirate's eye sockets glowed a dull red, and strands of dripping seaweed hung from his sword, his black hat, even his gold earring. She briefly admired the use of color and the delicate crosshatching before saying, "I told you, no ghost stories at bedtime. Now Gabriel will have nightmares."

"But Mom, it's not even scary," protested Tommy.

Gabriel sat up in bed with the pillow on his lap. "Can we sleep with the light on?"

"When I tell you to do something you have to mind me," said Lillian. "Now, did you both brush your teeth?"

Gabriel nodded and bared his teeth. Tommy whipped back the blanket, jumped up, and headed for the bathroom. "Whoops. I forgot."

"Thomas, you're old enough to remember to brush your teeth."

Lillian took a towel and oil cloth from the top dresser drawer. "Scoot over, Gabe."

Gabriel rolled to the side as she placed the cloth and towel in the middle of the mattress, and then covered him up. She sat down on the edge of his bed.

"I won't Mommy. I didn't drink anything late."

"Well, just in case. It won't hurt to have it there."

"How come I'm doing it? I'm not trying to."

"It's just a phase – the new place, all the new changes. Nothing to worry about."

Gabriel threw off the blanket and climbed onto her lap. She lightly rocked him.

Tommy jumped back into bed, pulled the covers up, and then leaned on an elbow. "Mom, Mickey said his dad said we're going to war."

"Oh, I hope it doesn't come to that." But her brow slightly creased as she smoothed Gabriel's hair. She remembered her uncles going off to fight when she was young and never coming back. How her grandmother was never the same.

"Well," said Tommy, "if it's still on when I'm older, I'm going."

"It's not a game, Thomas. War is terrible."

"Well, Mickey's dad said we have to stop Hitler. And that means war."

Lillian laid her cheek against Gabriel's head, unable to refute Tommy.

After a few moments of silence, Gabriel shifted to face her. "Mommy, is it almost Christmas?"

"It's right around the corner. We have a lot to do. How about tomorrow we start our paper chains and decorate the windows?"

"We can put up our snowflakes," said Gabriel.

"Can we get our tree tomorrow?" asked Tommy.

"And hang our stockings?"

"Whoa, slow down. Let's get started tomorrow and see how far we get."

Lillian glanced at the Christmas photo on their dresser. She and Tom sat with the boys on their laps, Gabriel just a baby, Tommy barely four. They were all smiling, but something had caught Tom's attention and he looked off in a slightly different direction. That tiny gesture always filled her with sadness – as if part of him had already left them. It was the only family picture of them all together, taken a few months before Tom died. She gazed at the photo and thought – Oh, Tom. Why did you have to be so impulsive and rush in? You should be here now.

Lillian felt the loss for her boys, and herself, even more at the holidays. Tommy and Gabriel clung to every image and story of him. She wished there had been more such photos and she made up for the lack of them by inventing stories about Tom for the boys. Any sense of guilt at doing so was lessened by her belief that she only made up stories that could have been true. She was careful to capture his true character, what she remembered of it. But sometimes she found herself confusing the invented stories with the real stories. Time had a way of blending everything together.

Tommy must have followed her gaze, for he now asked, "Mommy, remember the time Daddy knocked down the Christmas tree?"

Gabriel laughed. "I remember that."

Tommy jerked his head back in disbelief.

"You weren't even born yet!"

"So. I still remember it."

Tommy looked at Lillian, who subtly shook her head at him. He then grinned and handed Gabriel one of his books.

"Here, Gabe. This one has lots of pictures. Don't worry, Mom, no skeletons or ghosts in this one."

Gabriel took the book and climbed back under the covers.

Lillian kissed them goodnight. "Ten more minutes." She took the ghost story book with her.

"Night, Mommy," both boys said, already engrossed in their books.

Lillian curled up on the couch and browsed through the book, studying the illustrations. She then picked up her sketch pad and began to draw a picture of Tommy and Gabriel. She smiled as she heard them talking in pirate voices.

Tommy initiated it, as usual. "Yaargh! Long John! Look. He's found the buried treasure."

Gabriel did his best to sound like his brother. "Well, shiver me timbers!"

They sang "Fifteen men on the dead man's chest. Yo ho ho, and a bottle of rum!" taking turns starting and ending it.

The problem with Mr. Drooms, Lillian thought as she sketched the boy pirates at the helm of a ship, was that he didn't have any children to keep him grounded in life.

By the time her sons' voices died down, Lillian's sketch was nearly finished. She held the drawing at arm's length, and tilted her head. Then she gave them each a tiny moustache and goatee.

She closed her sketch pad, picked up her book, and tucked the afghan around her. Let's see, she thought. Where was I? Ah, yes. Dorothea Brooke and her emeralds.

Chapter 4

෩

Drooms was glad that the weekend was over and he could once again surround himself with Drooms Accounting and the busyness of meetings and decision-making and the plans to expand his accounts. When he arrived at his office on Monday, he was surprised to see Mason's chair empty again. He wondered if everything was all right. Mason was never late, and now he was twice in one week.

Drooms went to ask Mrs. Murphy for a particular file, but she was on the phone and he was impatient, so he went to retrieve it himself. As he browsed through the file drawers, he overheard some of the employees discussing Mason.

"It's not like him to be late again," said one of the clerks. "Do you know what's going on with him?"

The typist shrugged. "It's a busy time for him, I guess. You know he lives with the whole family – his mother and all those sisters. And now with his wife expecting again, they've moved to a larger place. I don't know how he does it."

Finch motioned for them to come closer and spoke quietly. "Don't let this out, but he's taking another job. He –"

Drooms dropped the file on hearing this. The others stopped talking and appeared deeply buried in their work as he passed them on his way back to his office.

He took the folder and tossed it on his desk, unable to believe what he had heard. Mason had been his right hand all these years. It didn't seem possible that he would take another job. Though, now he thought of it, Mason did seem preoccupied of late.

Drooms kept eyeing the clock as he flipped through the file. They must be mistaken. Mason wouldn't leave him. Had he not been fair? Hadn't he taught Mason everything he knew? Drooms went to the window and looked down at the busy street below. There must be some explanation. He would get to the bottom of this, have a talk with Mason.

His thoughts were abruptly interrupted when he spotted Mason across the street, shaking hands with his main competitor, Howard Henderson.

"Henderson! I don't believe it!" Drooms watched the two men for a few moments, then he quickly grabbed his hat and coat and left the office.

Mrs. Murphy called out after him. "Shall I tell Mr. Mason to meet you at Carson's, sir?"

"Tell him I don't need him!" he shouted from the hall.

*

Perhaps it was Drooms's suppressed anger that gave him an edge at the meeting with the prospective clients from Carson & Co. Whatever the reason, Drooms convinced them that handing over their accounts to Drooms Accounting was in their best interest, and he negotiated the deal nearly entirely on his own terms.

As he shook hands and left the meeting room, he couldn't help but smile knowing that he had so smoothly pulled off a deal they had been working on for so long. He felt a small pang of disappointment that he and Mason couldn't wrap it up with a celebratory lunch.

As he walked back across town, he congratulated himself. Yes, he still had what it took, and he could do without Mason, if it came to that. He might even consider expanding if things continued as they were going, hire two more accountants, another clerk perhaps.

He waited for the light to change at Fifth Avenue, dimly aware of the horns blaring, the shoppers gawking at the store windows, the swerve of taxis as they spotted a hand in the air.

Then suddenly, the vibrating world around him came to a halt, as he recognized the woman in the deep blue coat and hat across the street – his neighbor, Mrs. Hapsey.

There she was, walking along, glancing at the store windows that were decorated for the holiday. Drooms observed her as she paused in front of a large display of children's items – a red wagon, rocking horses, doll houses.

He decided to walk along Fifth Avenue and cross further down. Though he told himself that he had no interest in her whatsoever, he nevertheless found himself walking somewhat parallel to her, turning now and then to watch her.

He was just about to give up such foolishness when he saw a chauffeur-driven car stop alongside her. A man in a long fur coat stepped out and addressed her. Drooms recognized him as Randolph Rockwell, a man whose name and picture were often in the papers. Rockwell liked to toot his own horn about the charities he was involved with, though his reputation was that of a shrewd, and sometimes unethical, businessman – and recently divorced, if Drooms remembered correctly.

Drooms tried to interpret Lillian's response to Rockwell. She backed up a step or two but she was giving that smile of hers, with the little dimple and flash of white teeth. Drooms tried to make out what was happening next but the traffic was obscuring his view. It looked like Rockwell took her elbow and gestured to the car, but she backed up slightly and shook her head, pointing to the store. Then – damn the bus! It blocked his view, completely – and when it passed, she was gone. Did she go into the store, or did she get in the car with Rockwell?

Drooms shoved his hands in his pockets and picked up his pace. Women were always after men with money, he knew that well enough. Couldn't really blame them though, especially the ones with children. He scowled at his own thoughts. Something about that woman threw him off every time he saw her and he was beginning to get tired of it.

He forced his thoughts back to Mason and considered the next step he would take with Henderson, the snake. Can't trust anyone, he thought.

When Drooms arrived at his office, he saw that Mason was now at his desk. Drooms ignored him and instead addressed Mrs. Murphy.

"I want you to start an accounts file on Carson & Co." He smiled at her reaction. "I finally won them over to my way of thinking."

"Congratulations, sir!" she said, clapping her hands together. "I knew it was just a matter of time."

Mason stood, genuinely happy, and was ready to shake his boss's hand.

"Congratulations! All our legwork finally paid off. I'm sorry I wasn't there to see it, but I was –"

"I'm sure you had something important to tend to." Drooms disregarded the outstretched hand and walked up to Finch.

"Finch, I want you to take the lead on this."

Finch rose to his feet, pleased, but surprised. He looked from Mason to Drooms for further explanation, but received none.

"Yes, sir. Thank you." He sat down, uncomfortable with whatever was going on between the two men.

Mason stood silent with his mouth open. He was about to ask for clarification, but Drooms cut him off.

"Mason, I want you to give me the notes on the Henderson company. That should be easy enough."

Mason looked at Drooms, unsure of his meaning. "Yes, sir." He slowly sat down.

*

Drooms walked home, trying to recapture the feeling of pleasure over the deal with Carson &

Co., but the image of Mason shaking hands with Henderson bothered him more and more. As he approached the brownstone he saw his new neighbor up ahead, coming home from work. He remembered her fancy man in the limousine, and crossed the street to avoid her.

He couldn't care less about her, but he hadn't thought she was the type of woman to take up with someone like Rockwell; he even uncharitably wondered if Rockwell had bought her the beautiful blue coat. He would go straight to the diner tonight. Have an early dinner. Go home later.

Drooms took his usual booth at the diner, ordered the Salisbury steak and potatoes, and opened the newspaper he brought with him. Over his meal he replayed the deal he had just closed. It would bring in some healthy revenue. Yes, the Carson deal was a real coup. No need to give Mason, or anyone else, another thought. He was pleased that he could always count on his business. In all these years it had never let him down.

He returned home, his mood greatly improved by the fresh air and warm meal. He would focus only on the things he could be sure about. His work and…well, his work. That was enough.

*

That evening, Lillian began some of her holiday baking. The gingerbread loaf she had placed in the

oven almost an hour ago now filled the small apartment with its spicy aroma. She opened the oven
door and saw that the edges were browning nicely.
Another ten minutes should do it.

She took out the fruitcakes she had made
months ago, and drizzled a little brandy over the
cheesecloth. The holiday desserts were traditions
from her mother, and Lillian had not missed a single year of making them since she had left home.

Baking was an activity that usually relaxed
Lillian and gave her a sense of pleasure, but tonight
she felt tense, irritable. She couldn't shake the
image of Mr. Drooms purposely avoiding her just
as she started to greet him this evening. Was
he trying to be intentionally rude to her, or was
he that way with everyone?

She looked at the clock and put a hand on her
hip. And now Tommy and Gabriel were over
half an hour late. They had begged to play with
Mickey and Billy before dinner, and she had
given in. She took off her apron, annoyed that
she would have to interrupt her baking to fetch
them inside. She was just putting on her boots
when she heard them clamoring up the stairs. She
opened the door, and brushed the snow off their
coats as they ran inside.

"Tommy, I told you fifteen minutes! What's
gotten into you lately?"

"We were just playing. No one else's mom
had a problem with that."

Lillian opened her mouth, about to reprimand him for his cheeky response. Instead she took a deep breath.

"Take off your boots and go wash up for dinner," she said.

"Sorry, Mommy," Gabriel said. "All of a sudden it got late."

As she set Tommy's snowy boots outside the door, she saw Mr. Drooms climbing the stairs to their floor. She reached behind her to get Gabriel's boots, determined to avoid another rebuff from her grumpy neighbor. She promised herself that her attempts to befriend him were over. He obviously didn't want to be bothered, and she had enough to worry about without adding him to her list of concerns: the unwanted attention from her boss, being unprepared for the holiday, and Tommy's increasing antagonism. The last thing she needed was a tiresome neighbor.

As Drooms passed Lillian, he caught a whiff of fresh-baked gingerbread pouring forth from her apartment. The old familiar scent flooded him with an unexpected sense of well-being, and made him feel that he could afford a little neighborliness.

As he unlocked his door, he smiled and said, "You know, Mrs. Hapsey, your cooking reminds me of –" but when he turned, he saw that she had gone inside. He stared at her closed door, strangely disappointed.

Inside, Drooms took off his coat and hat and stood for a moment, as if he had lost his momentum, but from what, he couldn't exactly say. He would fix a cup of tea, clear his mind with a little work.

He filled the tea kettle, placed it on the stove, and then lit a match to ignite the burner. The faint scent of gingerbread found its way into his kitchen, again stirring up memories.

No point in remembering, he told himself. Best to keep busy.

He took the tea canister from the cupboard and spooned out some loose tea into a small wicker tea strainer. He placed the strainer in his cup, returned the canister to the cupboard, and added some sugar to his cup.

He drummed his fingers on the counter and checked the flame under the kettle. Rather than wait for the water to boil, he walked to the living room. Without turning on the light, he stood at the dark window and glanced down on the street below. Some older children were bringing home a Christmas tree on a sled. That image, along with the lingering aroma of gingerbread, put him right back in the old farmhouse kitchen, when he was twelve years old.

That Christmas. There was his mother bent over the oven, checking on the gingerbread. His older sister Kate, her apron white with flour, was rolling out cookie dough on the wooden table – giving a thump with the roller every time she placed it on the dough, just the way his mother did.

The twins, Sarah and Sam, six years old now, were running around the kitchen getting in the way. He knew they just needed some fresh air.

"Come on, you two. Let's go look for our tree."

How they had whooped with excitement. His mother threw him an appreciative smile over her shoulder.

But he had another reason for wanting to find the tree. It had been a few days since he had seen Rachel. The tree would give him an excuse to ask her brother Caleb for help chopping it down.

Rachel, his best friend ever since her family had moved into the neighboring farm four years ago. It had started with a competition of who could find the most interesting things to show each other: a rusty nail in the shape of a letter, an arrowhead from the newly ploughed fields, a molted snake skin from the woods. But after a few years, the competition vanished, and the little treasures became offerings to each other: a yellow-and-black butterfly in a jar that they would admire together and then release in the meadow; a robin's egg perfectly broken in half – Rachel's favorite color, *sky color* she called it; bouquets of bluebells in the spring, bunches of holly at Christmas. At eight they had been tree-climbing, frog-finding friends; at twelve, they were confirmed sweethearts.

The twins chattered while they put on their coats and boots. Then they pulled on their green mittens and matching hats with red tassels that Kate had recently knitted for them.

"I know just the tree," said Sam.

"So do I," said Sarah. "I'll get a ribbon to mark it so you won't forget the tree we pick." She clomped up the wooden stairs in her boots, and soon came back down with one of her red ribbons.

As they left the house, Kate and his mother stood in the doorway.

"This is going to be the perfect Christmas, Mother," said Kate, nestling her head against her mother's shoulder. "We even have snow!"

Then, just as he walked out the doorway, those words from his mother to Sarah and Sam:

"You two mind Charles, now."

He turned to his mother with an expression that said he was old enough to handle the twins.

She smiled and put a hand on his shoulder. "I know, I know. I can always count on my Charles."

Sarah and Sam had already run ahead to check on their baby rabbit.

"Now, stay in your pen, Alphonse," said Sam.

"And don't run away," added Sarah, shaking her finger at the tiny rabbit.

"Alphonse! Is that what you named him?" he had laughed.

"Cause he's so smart, Charlie," Sarah said, taking a bit of bread from her coat pocket and sticking it through the chicken wire.

Sam knelt down to check the latch on the makeshift pen. "He keeps getting away. We almost couldn't find him last time, Charlie."

"Well, we'll make a stronger pen when we get back. Come on you two. Let's go find our tree."

As they walked through the woods, he listened to the twins' plans to make a snow house, but he soon got distracted when he saw Rachel and her brother Caleb coming towards them on the path.

Sarah and Sam began singing, "Charlie loves Rachel, Charlie loves Rachel."

"Hush up!" said Charlie under his breath, as he ran a hand through his hair. He smiled when he saw Rachel's face light up like it always did when they met. Rachel, with her long dark hair, her sweet smile with the ever so slightly crooked front tooth, her blue eyes crinkling with merriment when she laughed –

The tea kettle's shrill whistle reached an ear-piercing shriek.

Drooms hurried to the kitchen and, with his hand shaking, he lifted the frantic kettle from the burner. His heart was pounding. He felt his pulse slow back down as the frenzy of the whistle lessened, lowered, and then vanished.

He poured the hot water over the tea, and took a deep breath. No point in remembering. The past is past. He lifted and lowered the strainer to steep his tea, up and down, watching the tea darken. He put the strainer in the sink and stirred the sugar at the bottom of the cup. No point in remembering.

He took his tea into the living room and placed it on his desk. Although a little ahead of schedule, he would study the monthly numbers. He always enjoyed comparing the books with his forecast, and then determining his next steps. It cleared, focused his thoughts. Once he began working, there was no room in his head for anything else.

Yet as Drooms settled into his desk, he realized that tonight his mind was fighting him. All those faded images were becoming sharp again, gaining in color and precision, against his will. It took more and more effort to suppress them, but slowly the numbers and columns and calculations took over.

Drooms was deep in his work, surrounded by stacks of papers and ledgers on his desk. Yet he kept shifting uncomfortably in his chair. Something. What was it? He inclined his head and frowned in concentration, listening.

He swiveled around and glanced over the living room, then to the inner room between his bedroom and living room. Just a closet, full of books, shelves filled with files of long-dead accounts, dusty old boxes full of junk. Nothing. Nothing there.

He returned to his accounts and tried to concentrate. But after a few moments, he again heard a tiny noise and looked behind him.

The doorknob to the inner room was turning.

He scowled, determined to ignore it. He took up his papers and stacked them loudly, repeatedly, and picked up his pencil.

Then he heard the door open. His shoulders slumped. Why? Why, now? He twisted around in resignation.

There he was – the boy with the red scarf. The boy pushed open the door and sauntered around the living room, examining the pictures on the wall, pulling the lamp chain on and off, glancing out the window.

Drooms shifted in his chair to keep his back to the boy, willing himself to focus on his work.

The boy moved about with a jaunty air, and then stood in front of the animal collection with his fists on his hips. His eyes opened wide when he spotted the new squirrel.

"A new one!" He petted it, and then examined it closely, comparing it to the other squirrel. "Hey, this one has gray eyes." He held up the other squirrel. "And you have brown eyes."

Drooms hadn't noticed this and scooted his chair back to see for himself. He lifted his reading glasses and compared the two.

Then he abruptly turned back to his papers, annoyed that he had paid attention to the boy. Drooms resumed his work, keeping his back to the intruder. He spoke softly but firmly.

"Put those down."

"I won't hurt them." The boy picked up the snake and flew it through the air, causing it to swoop around at the squirrels and the other animals. "And there's Alphonse!" he said, reaching for the rabbit.

Drooms snapped, and snatched the animals away from the boy.

"Leave them alone! And – go away! I don't want you here."

He put the animals back in their places and whipped around. Except for the animals, he was alone.

Chapter 5

❦

A few evenings later, just after dinner, Tommy and Gabriel decided to write their letters to Santa, and they wanted to make a celebration of it with a fire, and hot chocolate with marshmallows. But Lillian realized that they were out of all the ingredients, and had no more firewood; she would make a quick trip to the corner store before it closed.

Tonight she felt the fatigue in her legs from her years of working as a sales clerk. But as she put on her old blue coat, she thought that at least her job in the department store had yielded a few special items, like her blue coat and matching hat that had seemed such an indulgence at the time, a few pretty dresses, and some furniture she would never have purchased if it hadn't been for the discount.

As she walked to the corner store, she wondered if she would still have the endurance for department store work, for standing all day. The pointed attentions from Mr. Rockwell were beginning to worry her. She couldn't afford to lose her job. Not now. She had so wanted to make this a special Christmas, that she had allowed herself to place a few toys and clothes for the boys on layaway. Perhaps she could take in sewing again. She could ask Mrs. Wilson and Mrs. Kuntzman if they knew of anyone who might need some mending done. There was always some way to make a little extra money.

Lillian entered Mancetti's and purchased a few items, along with the milk, cocoa, marshmallows, and fire wood, deciding that after the holiday season she would have to find some places to cut back. As she left the store, she ran into Mrs. Wilson, who was just entering.

"Evening, Mrs. Hapsey. Having a fire tonight?"

"Yes. The boys are going to write their letters to Santa. Mrs. Wilson, I meant to ask you – I was wondering if you know anyone who might need some sewing done. It's something I used to do to make a little extra."

"Ah yes, with the Christmas season and all. I guess that pension doesn't get you very far, does it? Listen," she said, taking Lillian's arm conspiratorially. "Just you hold tight. There's talk about jobs opening up for women. Once this war starts, the men will be gone – and they'll need *us* to fill their jobs. And you can forget about ever doing sewing again. Mark my words."

Lillian sighed at the grim prediction. "The way things are going, it seems unavoidable. How terrible."

"It's the way of the world. Ah well, enough of us will survive the war to ensure that we may have many more. And on that cheerful note, I better get moving – Harry is waiting for his Epsom salts. Goodnight, dear."

The grocery bag seemed to grow heavier with each step. The threat of war. Fatigue. Worry. Fight it as she might, the world was often a lonely, unfriendly place.

Lillian frowned at the indulgence of such a thought. What were her problems compared to what the people of England were suffering? Over fifty consecutive nights of air raids on London in the fall – she couldn't begin to imagine the horror. And on Coventry last month. Who knew what was up ahead?

At least she had a warm home to go to. At least she could safely walk to the store and buy food, and her boys were happy and well-fed. No bombs were falling from the sky. She gazed up at the starry night. I must never take it for granted, she thought. No one knows what the future will bring.

She reached her brownstone and climbed the steps. At the front door, she fumbled with the bag of groceries and the bundle of wood as she tried to get a better hold on the doorknob.

Drooms had gone to the diner straight from work and was now returning home. As he approached, he saw Lillian struggling at the door. He hesitated for a moment, and then hurried to assist her.

"Here, let me help you, Mrs. Hapsey."

"Oh, no. I can manage." But the bag slipped from her grasp.

Drooms caught it and held it as she opened the door.

Lillian felt too tired to insist, and allowed him to help her. "Well, thank you." She never knew what to expect from him, but it took too much energy to hold a grudge.

"I'm going up anyway," said Drooms.

She wondered if he said that to make her feel better about accepting his help, or to diminish any meaning in his gesture. No matter. But as they entered the vestibule, Lillian became aware that this was the first time they had ever been alone together. She wanted to fill the space between them with words.

"The boys are going to write their letters to Santa tonight, so I thought we'd have a fire."

Silence.

They climbed the first flight of stairs. She tried again.

"There's nothing like a crackling fire on these cold winter nights." She looked over her shoulder for a response. "Don't you agree?"

More silence. Lillian waited a moment, and then gave a little laugh. "You're not one for small talk, are you Mr. Drooms?"

When they arrived at the third floor, Lillian heard a ruckus within her apartment and quickly unlocked the door. When she opened it, she saw that Tommy had Gabriel pinned down with his knee, and Gabriel was squirming and kicking back with all his might, shouting, "I do too!"

"You do not!" Tommy's face was flushed from his exertion to prove his point.

"Yes, I do!" Gabriel rolled over and broke free.

Tommy made a grab at Gabriel's leg but missed.

Gabriel ran to the couch, with Tommy right behind him. Tommy was just about to jump on the couch when Lillian grabbed him by the collar.

"What's going on!" she said, placing herself between the boys. "I can't leave you alone for five minutes!"

Then she saw that Gabriel had blood on his shirt and under his nose. "Oh, dear. Here, lie down. Put your head back." She hurried to the kitchen to get a damp dish towel.

She shook her head at Tommy. "Thomas Hapsey! I don't know what's gotten into you lately. You were supposed to be in charge."

Tommy crossed his arms. "He started it."

Gabriel sat up, ready to go at it again. "He did! He said I can't remember Daddy so I pushed him. But I can. How come he gets to be the only one who remembers everything? I remember the Christmas tree falling."

Tommy was ready to burst from exasperation. "But it's impossible! You weren't even born yet. That's what I'm trying to tell you!"

Lillian sat next to Gabriel and placed the towel under his nose. "That's enough. You're both going to behave. Now!"

That last emphatic word ended the argument.

Lillian inwardly berated herself for fabricating memories that didn't include both boys. The falling Christmas tree story was the result of a desperate moment when Tommy was five or six and she couldn't get him to stop crying. The dramatic tale was just the thing to capture his attention and quiet him. Tommy still recounted the way the ornaments rolled all over the place and how he – though only three years old – was the one to find them all, even the one under the couch, and how he and his father had hung them all back up.

Lillian saw that Gabriel's nose had stopped bleeding. She went to Drooms, embarrassed that he had witnessed the family drama. She took the bundle of wood from him, laughing a little, in an attempt to lighten the mood.

"Goodness, what will Mr. Drooms think?" She placed the wood by the fireplace, and then took a deep breath. "Now, how about I make some hot chocolate? Doesn't that sound cozy? You'll stay for that won't you, Mr. Drooms?"

One of Lillian's strategies after breaking up a fight between the boys was to keep talking, in order to ease the tension and get their minds on something else. But with part of her mind worrying what Mr. Drooms would think, she realized that she sounded scattered, nervous.

She tweaked Tommy's chin, and then unbuttoned her coat and hung it on the hall tree. "You know better, Tommy. Older brothers are supposed to take care of their siblings, not hurt them. Isn't that right, Mr. Drooms?"

Lillian reached for the bag of groceries from him. "Isn't that right?"

But when she looked at him for an answer, she saw that he had gone pale. He stood in the doorway, his eyes fixed on Gabriel lying on the couch.

His voice was barely audible. "Yes."

"Come in, come in, Mr. Drooms," she said, placing the bag of groceries on the table. She wondered at his response – surely he had seen children fighting before. Surely he wasn't so far removed from family life.

Gabriel was too wound up to lie still for long. He got up and brought the dish towel to the kitchen. "It already stopped a long time ago, Mommy."

"Boys, tell Mr. Drooms to come in."

Gabriel ran and took Drooms by the hand. "C'mon, I'll show you our pirate fort."

"Pirates don't have forts," said Tommy. "They have ships."

"Yeah, I mean our ship."

Drooms gently released his hand from Gabriel's. "I'm sorry. I have something to do."

"Mr. Drooms?" Lillian called after him as he walked to his apartment. His door shut behind him.

"Doesn't he want to see our ship?" asked Gabriel.

"Not now, honey." She closed the door and put an arm around each boy. "Come on, let's make the hot chocolate."

The boys ran to the kitchen. Tommy pushed a chair up to the cupboards. "I'll get the mugs out."

"I'll open the marshmallows." Gabriel reached into the grocery bag, opened the box, and plopped a fluffy white marshmallow into his mouth.

Tommy opened a cabinet and pulled out some sheets of paper and a tin of crayons and set them on the table. He chose a few crayons and lined them up, organizing them by color. "I don't like Mr. Drooms."

Lillian turned to look at Tommy, surprised at his comment. "Why do you say that?"

Tommy shrugged. "He's crabby."

Gabriel rummaged around the tin and pulled out some crayons. "Well, I like him," he said, with a hint of antagonism in his voice. He held up two green crayons, trying to decide between them. "Besides, he's nice when no one's looking."

"Let's have some music," Lillian said, turning on the radio. She poured milk into the pan and stirred in the cocoa and sugar. She didn't like that she so acutely felt Mr. Drooms's pain, whatever it was. She had her own worries. But she couldn't forget the expression on his face as he looked at Gabriel lying on the couch. So vulnerable. So sad. She hadn't thought such emotion was possible in him. She couldn't help feeling protective of him, of anyone who looked like that.

Gabriel sat with his knees under him, leaning forward on the table in anticipation. But it was taking too long. "Can we start, Mommy?"

She continued to stir the hot chocolate, not hearing him.

"Mommy! Can we start our letters? I want to color on mine."

"Hmm? Yes, that's a good idea. Maybe you can draw a Christmas picture."

Tommy had already started to draw on his paper. "I'm going to make a treasure map on mine."

"Yeah, me too," said Gabriel. Th e b oys s at across from each other, best of friends now, and drew pictures and wrote their letters.

Tommy looked up after a few minutes. "Mommy, I didn't give Gabriel the nosebleed."

"Yeah, Mommy, that just happened because," Gabriel said.

The tenderness in Tommy's face, the unwillingness he always had to hurt anyone, almost made her cry. "I know that, sweetheart."

She stirred the chocolate and thought of Mr. Drooms, of her own pain, of all the pain in the world. Sometimes she felt overwhelmed by it all, and feared the dark creature of despair that was always gnawing inside her.

The boys didn't know what to make of her silence. Gabriel looked at Tommy, then at Lillian, and back to Tommy.

Tommy made his voice sound cheerful. "We're having a cozy night, right Mom?"

Lillian poured out the hot chocolate into three mugs and set them on the table. "We certainly are."

She sat at the table with her hands around the hot chocolate and watched the boys stir the marshmallows, waiting for them to melt. After a few moments, she got up and took out another mug and filled it with hot chocolate. She forced a smile for the boys. "I'll be right back."

She took the mug down the hall and knocked on Drooms's door.

"Mr. Drooms, it's me. Are you there?" She waited expectantly, but didn't hear anything. "The boys wanted you to have some hot cocoa." There was no answer. She lingered a moment, hoping that he would accept this tiny gesture, just one human to another.

Inside his apartment, Drooms sat alone in the dark. He heard the knocking as if it came from far away. He knew that on the other side of the door was happiness and life, a foreign world to which he did not belong. He had long ago carved a hole in emptiness, his refuge that always awaited him, and he now sat there quietly. All was still.

A narrow shaft of pale light from the street slanted through the parting in the curtains and softly illuminated the animals. There they rested, frozen in a past of their own, forever enjoying their final moment of life, before whatever fatal blow had come to them. There they were. Old, dusty, removed from their own kind. And utterly alone.

Lillian returned to her apartment, the few steps down the hall seeming so far, as if she had left a long time ago. There were her boys, drawing made up worlds, chocolate moustaches above their lips, safely anchoring her to the day, the hour, the moment. Here was her life. No need to seek out anything else.

They paused in their coloring and saw the mug in her hand. "Doesn't he want it?" Tommy asked.

Lillian shook her head and set the hot chocolate down at the end of the table. She looked at their drawings and the beginnings of their letters.

"Look, Mommy," said Gabriel. "It's a map of the buried treasure by a Christmas tree. There are presents under the X and the pirate snowman is guarding it."

"That's wonderful, Gabriel! Oh, the snowman even has an earring." Her voice didn't sound right, sounded false. She covered it with a smile and stroked Gabriel's head. She looked over at Tommy, who was working intently on his drawing. "Very nice, Tommy."

Lillian went back to her seat and took a sip of the hot chocolate that she had left. She gave a slight start on seeing that there were four mugs, each at a seat. Staring at the fourth mug, she felt herself slipping, slipping. The carefully constructed scaffolding over the empty hole in her life collapsed, unexpectedly, leaving her to fall dizzyingly into her own despair. The dark animal that she thought was securely chained at the bottom of the pit was now thrashing its way out, clawing wildly in its anguish, lurching at her chest; soon it would release its long pent up howl.

She stood up shakily. "I'm going to take a bath. You'll be in charge, Tommy?"

"Aren't you going to drink your hot chocolate?" he asked.

When she didn't answer, he looked up, and watched her closely as she turned up the volume on the radio. She rested her hand on the counter, then the couch, the wall, as she made her way to the bathroom.

She closed and locked the bathroom door, and turned the faucets on full. Then she covered her mouth with her hand as she slid to the floor and leaned against the tub, her sobs covered by the sound of the foaming water.

Chapter 6

∾

Mrs. Murphy found herself thinking increasingly about her boss. He was always difficult around the holidays, but this year something else was going on with him. She didn't know whether she should be concerned or not.

As she went to the files, she passed his office and noticed that once again, he was staring out the window, lost in thought. She glanced at the clock and saw that it was 12:15. She knocked lightly on his door.

"Excuse me, sir, but aren't you supposed to be at the lunch meeting with Carson's?"

Drooms snapped out of his reverie and looked at the clock.

"If they call, tell them I already left."

He grabbed his coat and hat and dashed out the door – the first time he had ever been late for an important meeting.

His mind was wandering lately, thinking of all sorts of things. Remembering, imagining, wondering. Not at all focused as it usually was. As he wove his way through the crowded streets, he had to admit that he would never have been late if Mason were still involved with the account. He realized how much he had come to depend on him, and enjoyed his company – ever sanguine, offering alternative points of views, possibilities. Mason's way of thinking was quite different from his own. He couldn't blame Henderson for trying to take him away, though it galled him every time he thought of it. But he had decided against speaking to Mason about it. If Mason wanted to leave him, so be it.

*

Lillian and Izzy stepped off the elevator at the end of the day and passed Mr. Rockwell, who was returning from an outside meeting.

"Hello, Mrs. Hapsey, Miss Briggs." He addressed Lillian with an expression of concern. "Is your son feeling better?"

Lillian searched for, but couldn't detect, any sarcasm in his question. "Yes, he is. Thank you for asking."

"I'm glad to hear it. Well, good evening," he said, without his usual predatory manner, and he stepped inside the elevator.

"He's clearly interested in you, Lilly."

Lillian shook her head. She assumed he was simply trying a different tactic.

"Don't discount him," said Izzy. "He could be your ticket to the Art Department. And he's not as bad as he first seems. You know how some people put up a fake front to scare people away."

"Yes, I do know and I don't like it. How is anyone supposed to know what someone is really like? Why can't people just say what they mean? Why must everyone be so difficult?"

Izzy was surprised at the warmth of Lillian's response. "He's actually kind of nice," she said. "In the ten years I've worked for him I haven't heard of him do anything too bad. Nothing out of the ordinary, anyway."

"I don't like the way he makes me feel – the way he looks at me."

"Oh, that's just a stupid habit that comes from being handsome and powerful."

Lillian shook her head. "No. He's not a comfortable person. There has to be some engaging quality, something you're drawn to, that pulls you in –"

"Sounds like you have someone in mind."

"No, I'm just saying…I don't know what I'm saying. I think I'm just tired." She waved her hand to brush away her tangled thoughts. "The boys have been asking when we can get a tree. I think I'll stop by the tree lot on my way home and see what they have. See you tomorrow, Izzy."

Lillian made her way down the busy sidewalk, thinking how lucky she was to have Mrs. Kuntzman as a babysitter. She could take her time getting home tonight. She didn't feel like taking the bus. Her mind felt jumbled, unfocused. Not happy.

That was no way to be this time of year, she told herself. She would walk along Central Park and try to get her thoughts in order, muster up some holiday cheer.

Usually it was the tiny things that lifted her up when she was down – the glow of the first lamplights in the dusk, the smell of wood fire in the air. She gazed out at the park with its snow-covered paths, heard the soft clopping of the occasional horse-drawn carriage, saw the lights of the city sparkling through the bare trees – and waited for that surge of pleasure. But tonight the beauty of the park did not touch her. Tonight it just looked cold and empty.

When she arrived at the neighborhood Christmas tree lot, she saw that it was busy with couples and families carefully selecting the perfect tree, deciding between the wreaths and garlands, and lining up at the hot cider booth. The scent of cinnamon and pine filled the air, colored lights hung around the periphery of the lot, and strains of Christmas music came from the corner where a group of street musicians played. It was just the kind of place she would normally have delighted in.

She walked from tree to tree, considering the different shapes and colors. She stood in front of a sage-colored spruce and felt its prickly branches through her gloves. Then she moved to a row of shimmery, deep green pines. She took off her gloves and touched the long, supple needles; she leaned in, deeply inhaling the pungent fragrance. She could imagine one of these trees in her apartment near the couch, with the fire crackling, the boys sitting in front of it discussing what Santa might bring. She would come back for one of these, bring the boys, get them some cider. It would put them all in the holiday spirit.

For now, she would get a wreath with red ribbon and give it to Mrs. Kuntzman. As Lillian held up different sizes, she saw Mr. Drooms coming down the sidewalk. She took a quick breath and moved back among the trees, not wanting to be seen.

He walked along the snowy sidewalk with his steady, heavy tread, his head and broad shoulders bent down. She realized that he was deep inside his own world and would not notice her. As he approached and passed, she wondered what darkness filled his mind.

No, she thought. There was nothing they could do for each other. Nothing. She watched him until he turned at the corner and she could no longer see him. Then she paid for the wreath and went to pick up her boys.

Lillian climbed the steps to the babysitter's and knocked at the door. When it opened, Lillian held up the wreath.

"For you. I thought you might like it for your window or door."

Mrs. Kuntzman smiled and graciously accepted the wreath, taking deep breaths of the fragrant pine and saying, "Ahh," after each one. "Like the forest back in old country, when I was a little girl. Thank you, Mrs. Hapsey. I put this in the window to make the house cheerful."

Lillian caught a different tone in Mrs. Kuntzman's voice and observed her closely; she was smiling as usual, but there was a hint of sadness in her eyes. Lillian had never seen her like this before and worried that the boys had acted up.

"Have the boys been giving you a hard time?"

"Ach, no, no. They bring me happiness." She made a vague gesture to the outside world. "It's those others. Last week they throw a tomato at window, today an egg."

"Oh, that's terrible!" said Lillian. "I can't believe people can be so –"

"Why they do this to me? I been here long time. My son fought and died in the Great War. My only son. What more they want from me?"

"I'm so sorry. I didn't know."

The sadness on Lillian's face prompted Mrs. Kuntzman to pat her hand and say softly, "This is what happen with war. This happen with last war, too. I don't tell Tommy or Gabriel. They will find out soon enough how the world is." She mustered up a smile. "For now, we keep them happy."

Lillian nodded and pressed her hand. "Please call me if there's anything I can do."

"Thank you, Mrs. Hapsey." She was holding the wreath and smiling as Lillian and the boys left.

*

Before going to bed, Lillian checked on her boys, as she did every night. But tonight the words from Mrs. Kuntzman echoed in her mind:

"They find out soon enough....For now, we keep them happy."

Lillian gazed down at her sleeping sons. The light from the street softly highlighted their cheeks, their foreheads. She bent over them and watched the soft rise and fall of their chests, their innocent sleep.

Here they were, safe in their beds. No war as yet, no sickness. They were excited about Christmas, the snow, life. Yes, she thought, as she kissed their foreheads, these are the beautiful hours.

She vowed to do whatever she could to give her boys strong roots and happy memories that they could always carry with them near their hearts – should they ever need them for company in some faraway snowy trench.

Chapter 7

On Saturday, Lillian and her boys passed Drooms in the doorway as he was coming home and they were leaving to go out.

"We got our Christmas tree!" Gabriel said to him, too excited to note Lillian's eagerness to keep moving.

"Just now – and we carried it home by ourselves," added Tommy.

Drooms smiled at the boys, and then turned to Lillian. "You should have asked. I could have helped you."

Lillian interpreted the gentle expression in his eyes as the poor-widow-with-children look of pity. "Thank you. We managed all right."

"Yeah," said Tommy. "It wasn't that heavy. We're going to get popcorn and cranberries to string."

"Want to help?" asked Gabriel.

Lillian didn't want to intrude on Drooms any further. She wasn't sure which part of him she was more afraid of stirring – his unpredictable irritable side, or that heartbreaking vulnerable one.

"Mr. Drooms is busy, boys," she said, giving him a graceful way out. But when Drooms appeared to hesitate, she added, "Of course, you're welcome to stop by."

He seemed to be gauging her face, trying to determine whether she meant it, so she added, "You could join us for a bite to eat if you like."

She found herself warming to the idea of having him over. It might be a good way for them to get past the tension that always seemed to surface between them.

"And see our tree," said Gabriel.

"And help decorate it," added Tommy.

Lillian laughed at their enthusiasm and turned to Drooms for his response. But he now appeared preoccupied and looked away.

"Thank you, but I have some things to do tonight."

Lillian's temper flared and her cheeks flushed pink. "Mr. Drooms leads a very busy life. He doesn't have time for tree trimming and visiting. Come on, boys." She left without saying goodbye.

Drooms was taken aback by her abruptness. He watched them continue down the steps.

Gabriel smiled and waved. "Bye, Mr. Drooms!"

Tommy called back from the sidewalk. "You don't know what you're missing. It's lasagna tonight!"

Lillian was angry with herself for inviting him so impulsively, and then losing her temper. She didn't want him to think that it mattered to her what he did.

Yet she felt disappointed by his response. She had briefly imagined an enjoyable evening of simple holiday cheer. Now she dreaded that he might have mistaken her invitation, perhaps he even thought she was setting her cap at him. She groaned and promised herself, once again, to ignore her neighbor from now on.

Drooms stared after Lillian as she walked out of sight. He wasn't quite sure what had just happened. Surely she didn't really want him to stop by? She was just a warm, neighborly sort of person, kind to everyone.

He went upstairs and attempted to organize his papers, but couldn't seem to focus. After a few hours of fruitless activity, he decided to go to the diner. When he passed Lillian's door, he had half a notion to knock, knowing of course, that he never would.

Drooms sat at his usual booth, opened the menu that he knew by heart, and began to peruse it. The thought, the possibility that perhaps Lillian had been sincere in her invitation, struck him like a blow. What if she had really meant it? She certainly appeared offended when he declined. He tried to imagine himself sitting at the same table as her. What would they have to talk about? He felt both shaky and warm, almost happy at the thought.

He quickly dismissed such foolery, looked again at the menu and saw that he had been staring at the dessert page. He opened to the specials, but once again his thoughts drifted, and he imagined Lillian moving about her apartment. Was she clearing the dishes by now, trimming the tree? Was she thinking of him?

His gaze fell beyond the menu and into the dark wood of the empty booth. Never one for music, he was surprised to find himself lost in the simple lyrics of "Maybe." *Maybe, you'll think of me. When you are all alone.* He set his menu down and let the rest of the world fall away as he listened to the words, wondering at the desperate stirring in his heart.

The waitress came and asked him if he wanted the meatloaf special. When he didn't answer, she smiled. "You like the Ink Spots, sir?"

Drooms frowned at being caught in a personal moment. "When did you start playing music here?"

She looked around, perplexed. "You mean the radio? We always have it on."

He glanced down at the menu. "It must be on louder tonight or something. I'll have the special." He slipped the menu back in its stand and continued to frown as he tried not to listen to the song.

He ate his dinner, stopping to look out now and then at the lights and traffic and pedestrians. Everyone in a hurry to go somewhere. After dinner, he sipped his coffee and opened the newspaper he had brought with him. When he realized he was reading the same page over and over again, he asked for the check, and left.

*

Lillian and the boys sat at the kitchen table, which was strewn with strings of popcorn and cranberries. Gabriel hummed along with the Christmas music on the radio as he attempted to make a red and green paper chain, and Tommy decorated his paper snowflakes with bits of foil and sparkles from the crafts box.

Lillian quietly mended a blouse. She was thinking of other Christmases, and how Tom had always been in charge of putting up the tree. She should have paid more attention. After he was gone, his buddies from the firehouse had always delivered a tree and set it up for her. This year she had declined their help, saying that she only had room for a small tree and that she and the boys could manage. She didn't want to bother them any more. She no longer lived close to them, and they all had families of their own.

She lifted her eyes from her sewing and frowned at the mess in the living room. Near the couch a large box sat open, revealing Christmas decorations. Strings of lights were stretched out on the floor. The six-foot tall Christmas tree lay on its side near a stand, pine needles all over the rug.

Lillian shook her head and shifted her attention to the boys. Tommy was carefully picking out just the right bits of foiled paper and sparkles and then gluing them onto the largest snowflake. Gabriel was brushing paste on the end of a red strip of paper, his tongue in the corner of his mouth in concentration.

Gabriel pressed together the ends of the loop, waiting for the paste to hold. "Hey, I know. While the paste is drying, let's see if we can name all the reindeers."

Tommy sneered without looking up. "Don't be a dope, Gabe."

"Tommy!" said Lillian. "What have I told you about talking like that?"

"But Mom," Tommy said, "that would only take ten seconds. Dasher, Dancer, Prancer, Vixen, Comet, Cupid, Donder, Blixen. Five seconds. His paste is going to take at least a minute."

Lillian tried to sound stern. "That's beside the point. I don't want you calling names."

Gabriel gave a snort under his breath. "You forgot Rudolph."

"He's not really one of the reindeers," said Tommy.

"Yes, he is," said Gabriel.

"No. He's not."

"He is so. Right, Mommy?"

"Come on, boys. Enough of that. Finish up your projects. We're going to need your decorations." Lillian made a few more stitches. "This is our first Christmas in our new home – we have to make it look especially nice."

"I like our old home better," said Tommy.

"You just haven't given this place a chance yet, that's all," said Lillian.

"Can't we go back," he said, "just for a visit?" His tone had changed. He sounded like a little boy again, with a touch of longing in his eyes.

"Yeah," said Gabriel. "Let's go back and see everybody. And then come back here. I like it here."

Lillian smiled. "We will. After the holidays we'll take a trip. See all our old friends. How about that?"

Tommy shrugged and continued gluing bits of tin foil on his star.

"And now, a green one," said Gabriel. He carefully brushed paste on one end and squeezed the ends together. He rested his chin on his hand as he waited, and watched Tommy.

"I'm going to put sparkles on both sides of this one," said Tommy.

Lillian leaned over to look more closely at Tommy's progress. "Oh, how beautiful you've made it! All shiny and sparkling."

Tommy held up the snowflake by the string and blew on it to make it twirl. He nodded in approval and set it back down. "Just a few more pieces and it will be completely covered."

Lillian then switched her attention to Gabriel. "And look how long Gabriel's paper chain is. Very nice! Our new home is going to look so festive for Christmas."

Gabriel looked down at the paper chain and smiled at his accomplishment.

She thought of all the Christmases they had spent together and how quickly they had gone by. Then, as if picking up on her thoughts, Gabriel looked up.

"Mommy, will you tell me a Christmas memory?" he asked. Tommy was busy with his snowflake, but Lillian could see that he was listening.

Lillian put her sewing down and tried to remember the details of the stories she had made up, before repeating them. Every now and then the boys caught some discrepancy and weren't satisfied until she told it exactly the way they remembered.

"There are so many. Let's see. When you were a little baby your daddy would carry you to the Christmas tree and show you the lights and all the ornaments. And you would reach out your little hands to them. Especially the glass Santa. He was red and carried a green tree."

Gabriel delighted in hearing the tale. "That's cuz I liked that one, Mommy."

"Yes, you did."

Gabriel looked at her expectantly, waiting for more.

"And one Christmas, maybe you were two or three, I couldn't find you. I searched everywhere. Then I went into the living room – and there you were, fast asleep under the Christmas tree, with that same little Santa ornament in your hand."

"Yeah, I remember that. But Daddy wasn't there, was he. He was in heaven, right?"

Lillian picked up her sewing. "That's right."

Gabriel glued another link and pressed it together. "Is that where Santa is?"

"No, honey, Santa lives at the North Pole. You know that."

"I know." He thought about this for a moment, and then asked in a tentative voice, "But do you think he ever goes there?"

Both boys listened for her response.

She looked from Tommy to Gabriel. "Well," she said, setting her sewing down and considering how to answer. "I think he does at Christmastime."

Gabriel smiled. He then stretched out his paper chain across the table. "Finished!"

"That's beautiful, Gabriel!" Lillian leaned over and admired the uneven chain.

Tommy tied his glittery snowflake to the window latch. Down below he saw Drooms returning home. "Hey, there's Mr. Drooms."

Gabriel jumped up and knocked on the window and called out loudly through the glass. "Hi, Mr. Drooms!"

Lillian also went to the window and peered down. There he was with his hands thrust in his pockets, walking through the snow. Gabriel knocked on the window again.

"Don't bother him, boys."

Just then, Drooms raised his head. The boys waved to him. He gave the smallest of nods.

Then he stopped, and he and Lillian looked at each other, an intense charged exchange. She was glad there was a pane of glass between them, glad for the distance of two stories, glad that she was inside and he was out. Yet even with all those barriers, his gaze penetrated her heart, as if he had just placed his warm hand there and pressed.

She put a hand on the boys' shoulders. "Come on. Put your things away. It's time to wash up."

While the boys splashed in the bathroom, Lillian stepped over the garlands and boxes. She started to organize the Christmas mess, then gave up and sat on the couch, gazing at the embers from the fire they had made earlier. She heard Mr. Drooms come up the stairs, with his heavy slow tread, as if gravity rested its leaden hands on his shoulders.

Her sketch pad lay half buried under the boxes of tinsel and ornament hooks. She picked up the pad and pencil and turned to a new page. She stared at the whiteness, thinking of Drooms out in the snow. What was it about him that so pulled at her?

Lillian tapped the paper with her pencil, and drew a few tentative lines, and then began a sketch. An outline of him in the snow began to take shape. Yes, there he was – a man alone in the swirling snow, head down, trudging to some destination of his own. She studied the figure for a moment, then added icicles hanging off his arms, his hat, his coat – making him appear even colder and more forlorn.

She studied it for a moment, then closed the pad, and held it closely.

*

Drooms climbed the stairs to the third floor and when he passed Lillian's apartment, he felt his heart quicken, and he half expected the door to open. Then he realized there was no reason why this should be.

He entered his apartment, stomped the snow from his shoes, and hung up his hat and coat. When he turned, he saw the mischievous boy walking around the apartment as if he owned the place.

Drooms was about to chastise him, but decided it was better to simply ignore him. He would organize the stacks of paper on the kitchen table. There must be three months of papers he could file away.

But as he started to separate them, he found it increasingly difficult to concentrate. The boy had followed him there and was purposely getting in the way – rolling pencils under his palm, flipping through the ledgers as he stifled an exaggerated yawn, drumming his fingers on the kitchen table. Try as he might, Drooms could not ignore him.

Drooms gave up and went to the living room. He tried to settle into his desk, but the boy had followed him there as well.

Drooms kept his back to him and decided to work on his accounts reconciliation. It would require his complete attention. He opened the ledger in front of him, sharpened his pencils, and put on his reading glasses.

The boy bounced noisily on the couch and tossed a pillow up and down.

Drooms tried his hardest to become engrossed in the columns of revenues and expenses, but for the life of him, he could not concentrate. He coughed once or twice, took out a few more pencils from the drawer, should he need them, and began to add a column of numbers.

The boy strolled over to the animals on the bookshelves and spoke to them as he moved them around, standing the new squirrel on its head, putting the old squirrel in the robin's nest, and arranging the robin, weasel, and blue-jay as if in lively conversation.

"Be still," Drooms said quietly, but forcefully, without moving his eyes from the ledger.

The boy put the animals down, and bent to read the book spines on the bottom shelf. He lifted out a thick tome on Roman history and pretended to browse through it; then he slammed it shut, coughing loudly and waving his hand at the dust that was released.

Drooms flinched at the sound of the slammed book but kept his eyes on his work.

The boy walked to the desk and stood just behind Drooms, watching him add columns of numbers.

Drooms shifted in his chair so that he couldn't see the boy, and then he rolled up his sleeves, as if now, he was really going to get some work done.

The boy gave a sigh of boredom and went back to the animals. He picked up the rabbit and began petting it.

"You were the very first one," he said in a soft voice, as if speaking to his favorite. He took a few steps back so he could view all the animals. "Let's see. Then the blue jay, then the squirrel and owl. Or was it the mallard." Then, with a wave of his arm, he declared in a louder voice, "And now there's a whole world of dead animals!"

Drooms spoke in a louder voice. "Be still."

The boy set the rabbit down and sat quietly on the couch, watching Drooms.

After a few moments of silence, the boy said, in a rather sarcastic tone, "I don't know why, but the widow Hapsey likes you."

Drooms gave a little puff of disbelief.

"Well, she does," said the boy.

This actually made Drooms smile. "Ah yes, the beautiful, charming widow likes the old, dry-as-dust accountant." He tallied the numbers and entered the figure at the base of the column. "Highly unlikely."

The boy sat silently for a few more moments, then added, in disbelief, "*And* she thinks you're handsome."

Drooms took a sheet of figures and carefully compared it to the ledger. "Utter nonsense."

"So you don't believe me?" challenged the boy.

Drooms slid the pencil down the column, carefully checking his numbers. "Not for one moment."

"Okay – I'll show you. We'll just go and ask her." He jumped off the couch, ran to the door, opened it, bolted down the hall, and began knocking on Lillian's door.

Horrified, Drooms jumped up and ran after him. "No! Wait! Come back!"

Lillian had taken her bath and was reading on the couch when she heard the urgent knocking. She got up and opened her door – there was Mr. Drooms. She looked at him, and then glanced around the hall but saw no one else. She pulled her robe close and her hand went to the pin-curls in her hair. "Why, Mr. Drooms. Is anything wrong?"

"No, no." Drooms tried his hardest to appear relaxed.

They stood staring at one another.

"Did you come to see the tree?" asked Lillian. She turned to the disarray in the living room – the lights laid out on the carpet, the strands of popcorn and cranberries coiled on the coffee table, boxes of ornaments on the floor. "We haven't really done too much yet."

"No, no. I – It's just that – you were so kind to invite me to dinner and –"

"You're here for dinner?" She never knew what to expect from this man. She looked towards the kitchen wondering what she could throw together.

"No! No, of course not," stammered Drooms.

"I made some gingerbread the other day. Let me cut a few slices." Despite her recent resolve against him, she was happy he was there. And he appeared so ill at ease that she wanted to make him feel welcomed. "Please, come in."

She busied herself in the kitchen as Drooms watched her from the doorway. Feeling foolish just standing there, he reluctantly came inside and closed the door. He glanced around her apartment and felt even more awkward and self-conscious.

"How about a little sherry? Or port?" Lillian turned to ask.

"Oh, please don't trouble yourself."

Lillian pressed her lips together and gave a short huff of exasperation. Surely he didn't expect her to do this all on her own.

"Some port would be nice," he said, catching her look of frustration.

She took out a bottle from the cupboard and poured two small glasses. Then she placed them on a tray, and unpinned a few curls, trying not to be too noticeable as she fluffed out her damp hair.

Gabriel appeared in the hallway, rubbing his eyes. "Is it Santa, Mommy?"

From the boys' bedroom came Tommy's sleepy voice: "Santa doesn't knock at the door."

Lillian went to Gabriel and placed a hand on his shoulder. "Go back to bed, honey. It's just Mr. Drooms paying a visit."

"Hi, Mr. Drooms." Gabriel rubbed his eyes again and walked sleepily back to bed.

Drooms finally came to his senses. "I'm so sorry, disturbing you, waking the children. I really don't know what I was thinking."

Lillian set the tray of gingerbread, crackers, cheese slices, and two glasses of port on the crowded coffee table. "No, honestly, I just turned off their light." She gestured towards the couch. "Please, have a seat."

Drooms sat down stiffly, still feeling foolish. It was not like him to be so impulsive. Not like him at all.

Lillian pushed aside her sketch pad to make room for the tray, and handed Drooms a glass of port. She was glad the radio was on and that soft crooning filled the air around them.

Drooms waited for Lillian to take her glass, then lightly raised his glass to her and took a sip.

"I let the boys stay up a little later than usual tonight – they were so excited about the tree. And I always stay up a bit, until I'm sure they're asleep. I never know when I might have to vanquish a ghost or a sea monster."

Drooms gave an awkward smile and nodded.

Lillian waited for him to say something, but he remained silent.

She gestured to the garlands and lights strewn over the floor. "We didn't get too far, as you can see."

Drooms only now noticed the pine tree lying on the floor next to the stand. He looked at Lillian, then back to the tree. He hesitated, and then asked, "Why is the tree on its side?"

"Because it's a very stubborn tree."

Drooms set his glass down and got up to see what the problem was. "I can help, if you like."

Lillian stood but frowned at the tree skeptically. "I think it might need a different stand or something."

Drooms lifted the tree to an upright position and began to wedge it into the stand. "Here – if you hold it steady, I can secure it."

They worked together, making a few adjustments until the tree was firmly in place.

Drooms brushed the bits of bark off his hands, stood up, and took a step back to make sure the tree was centered. The corner of his mouth lifted in satisfaction.

Lillian clapped her hands, delighted. "Oh, the boys will be so happy. Thank you, Mr. Drooms."

They both looked at the strings of lights stretched out on the floor, and then at each other.

"Might as well," said Drooms. "It's much easier with two sets of hands."

Together they strung the lights, bending and reaching as they threaded the colored bulbs around and through the tree. Lillian was acutely aware of the nearness of their hands, felt the warmth from his arm as it lightly brushed hers.

She was encouraged by the words that flowed easily between them, now that they had a fixed purpose. He really was a pleasant man, when he wasn't scowling. He had a gentle way of handing her the lights, and he gave her a little smile each time he asked her to lift a branch, or hold the strand while he reached for it around the back of the tree.

She stole several glances at him while he was intent on the lights; for the first time, she was able to really see him up close. She tilted her head, and studied his profile, his mouth. There was an intensity to his eyes, always full of expression; now his dark eyebrows were lightly knitted in concentration. He was extremely handsome, with a strong brow and chin. She assumed he hadn't shaved since morning and the heavy shadow accentuated his angular features. She glanced at his arms with the rolled up sleeves, and quickly imagined his chest. When he bent to pick up the strand of lights, she noticed the thickness of his dark hair. It looked like there was a wave to it. Lillian imagined that when he came out of the shower it must indeed look wavy and –

Drooms looked up, feeling her eyes on him. She quickly turned and fumbled for the second string of lights on the other side of the tree. She gave her flushed cheeks a quick double pat, and took a deep breath. Then she handed the strand to him, smiling lightly.

He plugged one end into the other and with her help, looped the lights around the bottom of the tree. When they finished, Drooms searched for an outlet behind the tree. He bent to plug in the lights but Lillian reached for his arm.

"Wait!" She ran to the lamp and switched it off. Except for the light coming from the kitchen, the room was dark. "Okay. Now!"

Drooms plugged in the lights and the tree suddenly blossomed with colored bulbs, softly illuminating the room. They stood back, admiring their work.

"Oh, isn't it beautiful?"

"Yes, it is," he said.

They slowly sat back down on the couch.

Lillian reached for her port, and gave a warm smile. She clinked her glass to his. "To Christmastime, Mr. Drooms!"

Drooms raised his glass, took a sip, and smiled. Then he began to twist the glass around in his hands. "I wanted to say that – I didn't mean to seem ungrateful today. It was so kind of you to invite me, but I thought it would be an imposition to join you and the boys."

"Not at all. They've taken a liking to you."

Drooms's smile looked more like a wince.

"I'm afraid I'm not at my best around the holidays." He took a small sip. "Especially this one."

Lillian waited, wondering if he was going to explain himself further, but he remained doggedly silent.

She took a deep breath and reached for her glass. "It can be a difficult time of year. My sons always feel their father's absence more around the holidays."

Drooms turned to her, worried that he had caused her pain. "I'm sorry."

Lillian appreciated his concern, but didn't want any pity. She'd had enough of that over the years. "I'm not looking for sympathy, Mr. Drooms. We all walk around with some wound in us, don't we?"

Drooms glanced away. "I suppose we do." He wanted to stay away from this subject and guessed that she did too. He noticed the sketch pad and gestured towards it. "Yours? May I?"

Lillian handed it to him. "Of course. Something I do to relax. Nothing very impressive, I'm afraid."

He turned the pages, looking carefully at each sketch, clearly impressed. Lillian glanced over at the drawings as she surreptitiously hunted down a few missed pins and took them out of her hair.

He lingered over her sketches of Central Park: a twilight grove of trees with falling leaves, the Castle with a few imaginary winged creatures perched on the walls, the curved bridge over the lake filled with cattails and reeds in the rain. They were realistic and fanciful at the same time. He understood that she had a way of seeing the world that he had long ago lost. "These are very good. Did you study?"

"Briefly. A long time ago."

"This is something you should pursue." He smiled at the drawing of Tommy and Gabriel as pirates. "You've captured them exactly."

In a flash, Lillian remembered the sketch of him and reached for the pad, but he had already turned the page. He sat back, surprised to see the image of himself. Then he lightly scowled and held the drawing out at arm's length, clearly taken aback.

Lillian realized that the image could easily be misinterpreted as criticism, or even poking fun at him. "Oh, I'm sorry. I forgot I had –"

"This is me?" He lifted the pad towards the light from the kitchen and looked closely at the drawing.

"It's just a sketch. I didn't intend for you to see it." Lillian was uncomfortable that she had exposed her interest in him.

"Is *this* how you see me?"

"I draw what I see." She was angry with herself for not keeping her sketch pad in the drawer. And at him. What did he expect? Catching her unawares with this surprise visit, the place a mess, her hair in pins.

Drooms studied the drawing and nodded.

"Old, cold, and lonely. You're not one for flattery, are you?"

Lillian took the sketch pad from him and closed it. "Is that what you're looking for?"

"I'm not looking for anything."

"Well, you're the one who knocked at my door."

"And I see that was a mistake."

A glass wall rose up between them.

Though Lillian was hurt by his response, she was surprised that her words came out sounding so harsh, so defensive.

They sat in strained silence for a few moments. Then mercifully, the mantel clock chimed eleven. Drooms stood. "I had no idea it was so late. I'm sorry I disturbed you."

She also stood and watched him walk towards the door. "Mr. Drooms –" But when he turned to her, she lost her nerve and said flatly, "Thank you for helping with the tree."

Drooms opened the door, glanced at the tree, then back at Lillian. "Goodnight."

"Goodnight." She closed the door after him, brought the dishes to the sink, and turned off the kitchen light.

Then she went back to the living room, sank into the couch, and looked at the tree. The beauty and magic had disappeared. She unplugged the tree lights and sat on the couch, in darkness.

Chapter 8

Even though a day had passed since the evening with Mr. Drooms, Lillian was still upset on Monday morning. She felt irritable as she rushed to get ready for work, compounded by the fact that she hadn't slept well and as a result had woken up late. Her eyes required another layer of powder beneath them, which just added to her fatigued appearance. She saw that her blouse was frayed at the collar, so she quickly unbuttoned it and put on another one, keeping her eye on the time.

"Tommy!" she called out to the kitchen. "Are you and Gabriel eating your oatmeal?"

Then, just as she smoothed down her dress, she noticed a run in her stocking. She sat back down at her vanity in frustration and took out another stocking, quickly checking it for runs.

In an angrier tone she yelled out, "Thomas!" She hated it when he didn't answer her. "We have to go soon! Are you boys ready?"

She pulled off her stocking and put on the new one, then quickly brushed her hair, and applied some lipstick. When she passed the boys' room she saw that Gabriel had gone back to bed.

"Gabriel! Get up!" She pulled back the covers and roused him. "Come on. In the bathroom. Go wash up. We're going to be late."

Gabriel sat up in bed. "I'm tired!" He stumbled out and went into the bathroom.

Then Lillian saw that he had wet the bed again. "Oh, for heaven's sake." She stripped the bed, threw the sheets in the bathtub, and then went into the kitchen. There was Tommy, slouched at the kitchen table, spooning around his oatmeal with no apparent intention of eating it.

Lillian was ready to burst. "Can't you hear me? I've told you a hundred times, you have to help with Gabriel in the morning. He was still in bed!"

"It's not my fault if he went back to bed. I got him up."

"You have to do better than that. You're old enough to be more responsible."

"I can't help it if he doesn't listen to me." In an ear-piercing voice Tommy hollered, "Gabriel! Hurry up! We're gonna be late!"

"Stop yelling! That serves no purpose."

"You're yelling!"

Lillian could see a full-blown argument starting if she didn't hold her tongue. "Go help him get ready," she said quietly.

There were just enough leftovers from yesterday's dinner to make sandwiches for the boys' lunch. She added bananas and cookies to their lunchboxes, and then quickly buttered two pieces of bread, wrapped them in wax paper, and put it in a bag for her lunch. She added an apple, thinking, that would have to do.

In a few minutes, both boys were slumped at the table. Gabriel stuck his spoon in the middle of the congealed oatmeal. "I hate oatmeal!" he said. "I want to eat at Mrs. Kuntzman's. She makes good food."

Lillian grabbed the bowls and put them in the sink, banging them loudly. "Get your coats."

They all bumped into each other as they hurried to leave. Tommy took their coats off the hall tree and tossed Gabriel's to him. "It's this place. I hate it. I want to go back to our old home."

"Well, you're just going to have to get used to it," said Lillian. "We're staying here."

They walked to the babysitter's in silence, Tommy kicking at the snow along the way. The boys ran ahead when they saw Mrs. Kuntzman standing at the door waiting for them.

"Good morning, boys. I made crullers for youse. I hope you're hungry."

Tommy cast a sullen look at Lillian. "Starving."

Gabriel cried out, "Donuts! Yippee! Bye, Mommy."

"Be good, boys. I'll see you tonight."

Lillian watched them go inside without looking back at her. She waited a few moments to see if they would appear at the window, and then realized that they must have run straight to the kitchen. Tears started to well up in her eyes and she blinked quickly to prevent them from falling. She wished she could go back home and take a hot bath and just be alone for the day.

*

Lillian rushed into the office lobby, and impatiently pressed the elevator button. She bit her lip as she glanced at the large clock in the lobby; she had never been half an hour late before.

With the publishing office a whirlwind of activity, she thought perhaps she could get to the switchboard without Mr. Weeble noticing her. She walked past Izzy's desk, gave her a brief nod, and then ducked into the switchboard room. But within a minute of taking off her coat, Mr. Weeble walked in. He stood in the doorway, as if waiting for an explanation, and pulled back his cuff to examine his watch.

Lillian was not going to be intimidated by such a pompous, arrogant, stupid little man. Fed up with everything, she stood quickly, causing her chair to bang against the wall behind her.

"Yes, Mr. Weeble. What is it?" Her tone surprised even herself.

Mr. Weeble raised his eyebrows and blinked, looking more lizard-like than ever. Lillian half expected his tongue to dart out in search of a fly.

He raised his chin in an apparent attempt to look imperious. "Mr. Rockwell wishes to see you."

Lillian didn't wait for him to escort her this time. She stomped off to the president's office with a flustered Mr. Weeble trying to take the lead. Neither did she wait to be shown into Mr. Rockwell's office. She opened the door herself, leaving his secretary standing open-mouthed.

Go ahead and fire me, Lillian thought. I'm sick of all these games and those disgusting looks.

"Yes, Mr. Rockwell?"

Rockwell looked up in surprise. He sat at his desk, holding theater tickets in his hand, but was unsure whether to proceed.

Lillian saw his hesitation, and continued headlong into whatever fate awaited her.

"Mr. Rockwell, there's something you should know." She started to lose her courage and faltered a little. "I – I have someone. I've been seeing someone for quite some time." Lillian felt only a small pang of guilt at the lie that rolled so easily off her tongue.

Rockwell studied her, believing her this time, but was unused to being rejected. "And is it serious?"

Lillian swallowed and looked down at her hands. "Yes. Yes, it is."

"Well, then." He slipped the tickets into his pocket. "I'm sorry to have intruded. I wish you all the best." He took up some papers on his desk, signaling the end of the matter.

She started to say thank you but then changed her mind. He was the one who put her in an awkward position. No need to thank him for it.

She walked back to her station, determined to hold her emotions in check. The busy switchboard occupied her mind, though in between calls she mentally rehearsed applying at the department stores, hoping it would be easy to find a position during the holidays.

When she left for her lunch break, she saw that Izzy had followed her into the powder room. Lillian stood before the mirror, reapplying her lipstick.

"What was all that about earlier?" asked Izzy.

Lillian shook her head. "I think I just got myself fired."

Izzy gently pressed for more information. "You looked upset when you came in late this morning. Is everything okay?"

Lillian took a deep breath, unsure of how to explain herself. She closed the lipstick and twisted the tube around in her hands.

"I had an argument with Tommy. I seem to be snapping at everyone. Tommy, now Mr. Weeble. And Mr. Rockwell." She hesitated a moment and added, "Even my neighbor." Lillian buttoned her coat, annoyed that Izzy managed to bring up exactly what she didn't want to talk about.

"I had a feeling it might have something to do with him." Izzy crossed her arms, eager to hear more.

"No, it's nothing like that. At all. He helped me with the Christmas tree and we talked briefly. Then I insulted him and he left. End of story." She put her lipstick back in her purse and snapped it shut.

"That can be smoothed out," said Izzy.

Lillian shook her head and leaned against the counter. "No, Izzy. We're too different. Yes, he's handsome. And I thought maybe we could be friends. But somehow we aren't clicking." She started to leave. "It's just as well. I can't take on anything more. I really just need to slow things down and focus on the boys. And Christmas. I'm going to get some air. Want to join me?"

"Sure," said Izzy.

As they cut through the lobby, Lillian continued her thoughts. "At one moment he's so kind and warm – "

"Mr. Rockwell?"

"No, Izzy, my neighbor. Mr. Drooms. And then he closes up and I don't know what to think. But the last thing I need is someone who's going to make things harder."

"Well," said Izzy, "welcome to life."

Lillian looked up at the unexpected response.

Izzy spoke in a softer voice. "It's Red. He's going to Canada after the holidays. To enlist."

Lillian put her hand to her mouth. "Oh, my God. Izzy, I'm so sorry."

"Yep. He and his kid brother are joining the Royal Canadian Airforce. Red says Hitler has to be stopped." She shrugged and took Lillian's arm as they left the building. "Let's go grab a bite to eat, do some window shopping."

Lillian squeezed her friend's arm and felt guilty at her own petty problems. She would do what she could to cheer Izzy.

*

Drooms's bad temper from the weekend lasted into Monday and increased as the day wore on. Everything was a source of irritation. Finch wasn't handling the Carson transaction as smoothly as Drooms had expected, and he realized that he should have had Mason involved, even if it was just to guide Finch through the complexities of the deal.

After the employees left for the day, Drooms decided to check on Finch's progress. He went to the file cabinets, then back to his office, then back to the files in search of the Carson folder. He cast a suspicious look at Mason's desk. Surely Mason wouldn't have taken the information on Carson. Drooms started to rummage through Mason's drawers, slamming them in his search.

Mrs. Murphy, always the last to leave, was slipping on her coat when she heard the commotion. She came over and saw Drooms pulling open drawers and then shutting them with a bang.

"Goodness! What is it, sir? What is it you're looking for?"

"The file on Carson. It's missing."

"Why would Mr. Mason have it?"

Drooms crossed his arms. "I have reason to believe that Mason is going to work for Henderson."

Mrs. Murphy laughed outright. "Mr. Mason? He would never be disloyal to you. What on earth gave you that idea?"

"Look, I know he's taken another job. And I believe he's going over to Henderson."

Mrs. Murphy looked down, and slowly shook her head as she pulled the gloves from her pocket and put them on.

"He doesn't want anyone to know this, but seeing that you suspect him of perfidy – Yes. He's taken a second job. At Gimbels, working nights."

"I don't believe it! Doing what, for God's sake?"

Mrs. Murphy adjusted her hat. "Stocking shelves, helping with displays, whatever they need him to do."

"Why on earth would he do that?"

"To make it a good Christmas for his family, I suspect. Money is tight. You know he had to move to a larger place, and his wife is expecting again. And he dotes on those twins of his; he would do anything for them."

"Mason has twins?"

"Yes. But you knew that. And Gimbels gives him a nice discount. So there you have it. It's only for the holiday season, sir. He may be tardy now and then – but he's no turncoat."

"No. No, of course not." Drooms wondered why he had so easily doubted Mason.

Mrs. Murphy walked over to Finch's desk and immediately spotted the folder on Carson.

"Here it is, sir. Right where it should be."

Drooms leaned against the desk, ashamed of his suspicions. "I haven't quite been myself lately."

Mrs. Murphy gave a little chuckle. "That could be a good thing." She slipped her handbag over her wrist, tugged her gloves for good measure, and started to leave.

Drooms gave a slight smile at her ever forthright opinions. "Mrs. Murphy?"

"Yes, sir?"

"How long has it been, since Mason came here?"

"Almost twenty years. Same as me."

"Has it been that long? It seems like just yesterday I put him on the Whitmeyer account."

"Why, that was over ten years ago. When Alfred was still here."

Drooms stared at the floor, wondering how ten years could have passed without his noticing. How was it he could account for every penny, every rise and fall in revenue, but fail at the simple arithmetic of years gone by?

Mrs. Murphy looked curiously at her boss, wondering what had caused this recent disturbance in his equilibrium. He was often difficult, that was nothing new; but he had always been grindingly predictable. Lately, she never knew what to expect from him. She sensed some underlying change stirring deep within him. Something or someone had really gotten to him. Cantankerous as he often was, she couldn't help feeling protective of him.

"Will there be anything else, sir?" she asked in a gentle voice.

Drooms looked up from his reverie. "No, thank you. Goodnight, Mrs. Murphy."

Chapter 9

∽

The entire week was a struggle for Lillian. After work each day, she went to the department stores to apply for work, only to find that they had already done their hiring for the holiday. She arrived home late every night, leaving no time to spend with Tommy and Gabriel. Just a quick dinner before bedtime. Her apprehension had spilled over onto the boys and they were grumpy and irritable, especially Tommy. All week he pestered her about going back to Brooklyn for a visit, but she kept putting it off, saying now was not the time.

By week's end, Mr. Weeble still had not called her in, and she began to think that maybe she would be able to keep her job, despite what had happened. Or maybe they were just waiting to fire her in the new year. She would have to be prepared to take in sewing again. On Friday, after dinner, she got out her sewing basket and checked the contents, to see what she needed to add to it.

Tommy lay on the couch reading. Gabriel sat cross-legged in front of the radio listening to the *Lone Ranger*, alternately bouncing up and down to the music on his imaginary horse, then sitting spellbound. Tonto was just about to be jumped by a mountain lion when Tommy got up from the couch and shut off the radio.

"I'm trying to read." He went back to the couch and stretched out.

"Hey!" Gabriel got up and turned the radio back on and stood guarding it with his arms crossed.

When Tommy got up again, Gabriel yelled, "I was listening to my show first!"

Lillian had been trying to untangle the spools of thread in her sewing basket, and was growing impatient. "Tommy, go in your room if you want to read. Gabriel is listening to his show."

"I want to read out here." He started to shove Gabriel out of the way, and Gabriel pushed him back.

Lillian jumped up quickly to break the boys apart, knocking over her sewing basket and all its contents onto the floor. "That's it, Thomas! I've had enough of you. Go and clean your room!" She shut off the radio. "Gabriel, go wash up!"

"I didn't do anything! That's not fair," protested Gabriel. Then his face crumpled into tears.

He threw his arms down to his side and stomped off to the bathroom. "Now I don't know what happened to Tonto!"

Tommy went into his bedroom and slammed the door. "I always get blamed for everything!"

Lillian felt she was failing on all fronts. She picked up the spools of thread, the needles and scissors, the tape measure and chalk, wondering why everything was falling apart. Her vision blurred and a few tears fell as she ran her hands over the floor, feeling for any needles or buttons she might have missed. She knew that she had overreacted to the boys' quarrel, but sometimes she just couldn't hold it all in. She had so wanted this to be a good Christmas. Now it looked like it would be marred by constant arguments.

She put the supplies back into her sewing basket. Disconsolate and weary, she stood by the kitchen window and gazed down at the empty street below, thinking that perhaps they should have stayed put in Brooklyn after all.

*

The snow began to fall again the next afternoon. When Drooms walked home from his Saturday half-day, he saw Lillian and Gabriel outside the apartment building. Drooms was determined to ignore her but when he got close, he noticed the worry in her eyes.

Gabriel ran up to him. "Hi, Mr. Drooms. Tommy ran away, but he'll come back."

Lillian took Gabriel's hand and pulled him beside her. "He didn't run away." She turned to Drooms. "Have you seen Tommy?"

Drooms spoke gently. "No, I haven't. What happened?"

"He went out after lunch to play, but no one has seen him. He was angry with me from yesterday – and I don't know where he is. And it's going to be dark soon."

Just then she saw Mickey and Billy running up the steps to their apartment building. "Mickey, Billy – have you seen Tommy?"

"I saw him this morning at the store," said Billy. "Why? Is he in trouble?"

"I just saw him about an hour ago," Mickey added. "He asked my dad what train goes to Brooklyn."

Lillian covered her mouth. "Oh, my God!"

"That's where we used to live," Gabriel explained.

Drooms gazed down the street, ever so slightly crinkling his eyes, as if weighing something.

Lillian saw his look of distraction and was sorry she had confided in him. He obviously didn't want to be bothered. She quickly took Gabriel's hand. "Come on, we have to go."

She started to leave but Drooms placed a hand on her shoulder. "I'll go," he said.

Lillian shook her head, not trusting herself to speak.

Drooms spoke softly but convincingly. "What if Mickey is wrong? You have to stay here in case he comes back. Ask at the store, then go home and wait for him."

She hesitated, knowing he was right.

Drooms tried to reassure her. "If he's in Brooklyn, I'll bring him home. What's the address?"

Lillian closed her eyes for a moment. "It's gone. They tore down our building."

Drooms quickly read the worry in her eyes. "And Tommy doesn't know," he said, understanding her fear.

She slowly shook her head as she searched in her bag for something to write on. She found an old grocery list and wrote down the address and her phone number on the back of it, her hand shaking as she gave it to him. "Call me."

Drooms nodded and hurried off. Lillian watched him until he rounded the corner, then she went to Mancetti's store with Gabriel. Mrs. Mancetti had seen Tommy in the morning, but not since then.

Lillian stopped by Mrs. Kuntzman's and buzzed Mrs. Wilson, but neither of them had been outside and so they hadn't seen Tommy.

Lillian walked to the library and up and down the neighboring streets, but there was no sign of Tommy.

She took Gabriel home and pulled a chair in front of the telephone. Her sister Annette had convinced her to get one installed. Thank God she had listened to her. How she wished her sister was with her now. Lillian sat staring at the telephone, a tight knot in her stomach.

Gabriel leaned against her and she put her arms around him.

"Don't worry, Mommy. Mr. Drooms will find him."

*

Drooms rode the train to Brooklyn, growing nervous at the thought that he might not be able to find Tommy. What if Tommy had gotten off at the wrong stop, or taken the wrong train? Drooms didn't like being responsible for people, especially children. But then he remembered Lillian's face, her quick breathing, her worried eyes casting about as she spoke. He would have done anything to help put her at ease.

He looked down at the address she wrote, at the letters and numbers, and tried to find some clue to her in the loops and curves. Then he turned it over and read the grocery list she had written: *shoestrings, Ovaltine, soap, butter, eggs,* then *raisins* and *chocolate chips* – both with question marks after them. What did she mean? Was she deciding between two recipes? He wanted to know. He pressed the piece of paper between his palms.

The train seemed to take forever, full of innumerable stops. It had been a long time since Drooms was last in Brooklyn and he found that his memory of the streets was a bit jumbled. First, he got off at the wrong stop, then he later got turned around and had to backtrack.

He finally found the right street, and walked down several blocks, checking the address. When he realized he was on the right block, he looked across the street where the address should have been; the empty lot lay ruined with piles of rubble. A bulldozer, a few dumpsters, and scattered bricks were gradually being covered by snow.

Drooms looked around for Tommy and feared that he had already come and left, or, God forbid, was now lost, and wandering around in the cold. Then up ahead, between two parked cars, Drooms saw a lone figure, standing still among the falling snow.

There was Tommy, staring at the gaping hole where his home used to be. For one brief moment, it was as if Drooms were seeing himself on that cold December day long ago: there he was again, under the heavy gray sky, a dome of bleakness over the family plot, the utter stillness of the day. Nothing moved except the stinging snow as he stood there, immobile, frozen.

Drooms saw the same relentless flurries now swirling around Tommy as he stared at the snowy emptiness; only a lone stoop remained standing. He recognized the expression on Tommy's face as that of loss, for something that was gone forever, irretrievable.

Drooms slowly approached Tommy, and as he got closer, he could see the streaks on his cheeks, the eyelashes still wet with recent tears. Drooms felt a knot of anguish in his stomach, and wanted to smooth away the boy's pain. He gently placed a hand on Tommy's shoulder. "Come on, Tommy. Let's go home."

Tommy snapped around and shook off his hand. "Leave me alone! You're not my father!"

Drooms was thrown by the unexpected response. In an instant, Tommy had gone from vulnerable child, to angry boy.

Drooms suddenly doubted himself. Perhaps he was intruding where he shouldn't.

"I'm here because your mother was worried. You shouldn't have run off like that."

"Yeah, well she shouldn't have run off like that either. She just left our house, our home." His voice began to break, and he had to muster up more anger to finish his thought: "And she didn't even tell me why!"

Drooms thrust his hands in his pockets and looked at Tommy, then over at the empty lot, then up at the sky. He didn't know how to fix this.

"They tore down our house, and Mom knew. Every time I asked to come back she made an excuse. Now I know why." Tommy crossed his arms and set his chin at Drooms. "She should have told me!"

Drooms saw in Tommy a hurt child who was learning the hard lessons of life. How he wished that life could be kinder, could wait a few more years before placing its heavy burdens on children.

"Yes, she should have told you. You're old enough to understand."

Tommy had expected a fight, but now that Drooms appeared to be on his side, his face softened, and he once again became a little boy trying to understand why his world had crumbled.

"It's all gone. Everybody's gone." The only person he could find to blame, or knew to blame, was his mother. "She should have told me," he said again, but this time it sounded more like a plea.

They stared across at the rubble, watching the snow fall. Tommy roughly wiped his eyes and took in a few staccato breaths.

"She's doing her best," said Drooms.

"She never understands. Nobody does."

Drooms knew there was no consolation, no words that could fill that gaping hole in front of them. All he could do was try to soften the blow for Tommy, attempt to connect with him.

"You know, my father died when I was about your age, maybe a little younger. And I became the man of the house, too. I know it isn't easy."

Tommy didn't want to like Mr. Drooms, but at least he never treated him like a little kid. And now Drooms was telling him something personal about himself. Maybe he wasn't so bad. Tommy studied Drooms's profile against the gray sky, wanting to hear more.

Drooms kept his eyes on the lone stoop. "I had just turned eight."

"I'm nine. Almost ten." Tommy gazed out at the lot, then back at Drooms. "How did he die?"

"One day his heart gave out while he was working the fields. I was bringing his lunch to him and found him there."

Tommy felt bad for Mr. Drooms. "My dad died fighting a fire," he said softly. "I was four."

"He must have been a very brave man."

Tommy nodded and stood silent for a few moments.

"Mommy thinks I remember him, but I really don't." He abruptly turned to Drooms, alarmed at the words that had just come out of his mouth. He had often thought them, but had never spoken them to anyone. His eyes searched around, as if looking for an explanation.

"I mean – I want to. I try to. Sometimes I think I do. But then I know that it's really just the pictures and stories Mommy tells us. That's all I remember. Not the real him." His face took on a worried expression.

"But don't tell Mom," he said in a lower, protective tone. "It would make her feel bad." He shifted his weight and rubbed his arms, becoming aware of the cold.

Drooms felt his heart breaking for the boy. This poor child didn't even have the memory of his father, and if that wasn't enough, he had the burden of pretending that he did. That was too much for a nine-year-old. He once again placed a hand on Tommy's shoulder. "Come on. Let's go home."

They walked in silence down the street back towards the subway. Drooms wanted to get him inside a warm place.

Tommy kicked at the snow along the side-walk. "I bet you didn't have a little brother you always had to take care of."

"I did. And a little sister."

"Mom treats me like a baby, and then makes me do everything. It's not fair."

"Life hasn't been fair to your mother, either, has it? She has to be both mother and father, and it's not easy. She needs you, Tommy. And so does Gabriel."

"I know." He winced a little. "You think she's worried?"

"I'll call her and tell her you're with me."

Across the street, he saw a café with a phone booth inside. "How about some hot chocolate before we go back?"

Tommy hadn't expected this turn of events, and when he saw where they were going his face lit up.

"Hey, that's Saporito's. We used to go there all the time, especially in summer. Me and Gabe would have floats and banana splits and sundaes. Mommy always got a chocolate egg cream."

"Let's go inside. I'll give her a call."

They moved from the cold and gray of the street, to the warmth and liveliness of Saporito's Café.

The cafe was dominated by a large, carved mirror that ran the length of the counter, doubling the holiday lights and decorations, the booths full of customers, the children gazing at toys, the waitresses bringing phosphates and malts and sandwiches from the kitchen to the tables.

From a phonograph behind the counter, a scratchy Italian aria swelled and fell, reaching above the laughter and conversation and clinking of dishes.

Tommy scanned the counter and booths for any of his old buddies but didn't see anyone he knew. Then he saw Mr. Saporito behind the counter, weaving his hand back and forth to the music as he rang up a customer.

Tommy jumped up on a stool at the counter and tried to catch the owner's eye. "Hi, Mr. Saporito!"

"Well hello, Tommy!" Mr. Saporito mussed Tommy's hair and leaned on the counter. "I haven't seen you in a long time. I heard that you moved away. How's your mother? How's Gabriel?"

"They're fine. We moved to Manhattan. Central Park is only two blocks from us. We go there all the time."

Drooms took off his gloves and rubbed his hands, smiling at the owner. "How about two hot chocolates." He noticed Tommy reading the ice cream menu above the counter. "Anything else, Tommy?" He saw his hesitation and encouraged him. "Go ahead, get what you want."

"Can I have a hot fudge sundae, too?"

Drooms smiled. "Make that two," he told the owner. "I'll be right back, Tommy."

As he waited for the phone booth, he could hear Tommy filling in Mr. Saporito on their new home. Tommy was once again all exuberance and high spirits, making half twirls on the bar stool as he spoke, never still for a moment.

When the phone booth opened, Drooms went inside, fished out a coin from his pocket and placed his call to Lillian.

"Yes, he's right here with me. He's fine. Mrs. Hapsey?" For a moment he thought the line went dead, then he realized that she was crying.

"Everything's fine. We're just going to stop for a cup of chocolate to warm up, and then we'll head home."

"Thank God he's all right," said Lillian. "What was he thinking of, running off like that. Thank you, Mr. Drooms. Thank you for finding him."

The relief and gratitude he heard in her voice filled him with a happiness he hadn't known in a long, long time. Everything seemed so simple, so easy.

Drooms joined Tommy at the counter and took a bite of his sundae. "Pretty good."

Tommy twisted his spoon around, and lifted his face to Drooms. "Is she sore at me?"

"Well, first she was relieved. Then upset. By the time we get home, she'll just be glad to see you." Drooms took another bite. "Eat slowly."

Tommy smiled. "Thanks, Mr. Drooms."

Two boys about Tommy's age and a little girl walked in. One of the boys punched Tommy on the arm. "Hey, Tommy!"

"Hey, Dominic!" said Tommy. He saw Dominic's little brother and sister. "Hey, Tony. Hi, Mary." Tommy turned to Drooms. "These are my friends." He swiveled on the bar stool and pointed to Drooms. "This is Mr. Drooms. He's our new neighbor in Manhattan. I'm just showing him around the old neighborhood."

Drooms let Tommy visit his buddies, smiling inwardly at the conversation. Tommy's description of the city, his new school, Central Park, and the food his babysitter made caused the boys to cry out in envy: "Jeez, you're lucky!"

Little Mary said simply, "Golly!" to everything.

Then Dominic waved to someone in one of the booths in the back. "Well, there's my ma. Guess we gotta go now."

"Say hey to the guys for me," said Tommy. "I'll be back soon for another visit."

"So long," said Dominic.

"Bye, Tommy," said Mary. "Tell Gabriel I still love him."

Tommy cast a side look up at Mr. Drooms after they left. "I kind of fudged the truth a little bit. Hope you don't mind."

"You *are* showing me the neighborhood," Drooms said. "I'm glad I got to see it."

As they finished their ice cream, Tommy kept spinning on the stool, checking out the toys displayed across the aisle.

Drooms followed Tommy's gaze. "You like baseball?"

"I think so. I've never been to a real game."

Drooms walked over and picked up a glove and ball. He handed the glove to Tommy. "Here, see if it fits."

Tommy looked at the glove in disbelief, and then up at Drooms.

"Go on, give it a try," said Drooms.

As they left the store, Tommy hollered out to the owner. "So long, Mr. Saporito! See you later." Tommy glanced back at his buddies, glad to see they were watching. He gave them a big wave, wearing his new baseball glove.

Tommy was transformed as they set off to the subway station. "Thanks for coming to get me, Mr. Drooms. That was swell! Hey – catch!" Tommy mimed catching a ball and then throwing it to Drooms.

Drooms mimed barely catching the ball and hurling it to first base. "He's out!"

Tommy ran down the subway stairs laughing. All the way home, he tossed the ball up and down and punched his glove with it, talking non-stop about the stickball games they used to play in the old neighborhood and how some of the boys went to real baseball games. He described the summers up at his aunt and uncle's orchard, the train ride there, how they went swimming in the creek, and sometimes roasted hot dogs and marshmallows over a bonfire at night.

Drooms, in turn, told stories of the games they used to play on the farm, throwing horseshoes, jumping from the hayloft, and the animals he took care of.

"Wish I could live on a farm," said Tommy.

"But then you wouldn't know how to play stickball, or how to ride on a subway, or be able to get hot fudge sundaes at Saporito's."

Tommy laughed and punched his glove. "Yeah. I guess I like living here."

*

Lillian had been watching from the kitchen window, and when she saw Drooms and Tommy return, she ran down the stairs to meet them, with Gabriel following her. She knelt down and embraced and kissed Tommy. "Oh, Tommy. Thank God, you're back."

Tommy was embarrassed by her show of affection and backed up a little from her embrace. He had felt so grown up all afternoon, and now here she was, treating him like a baby again.

Lillian winced, as if Tommy's gesture had caused a sudden pain. She stood up and faced Drooms, and spoke in a voice that she hoped was steady. "Thank you for bringing him home."

Tommy and Gabriel ran up the stairs. Gabriel had seen the glove and was shouting, "Hey! Let me see it."

Lillian and Drooms followed in silence.

At their door, Tommy looked back and felt bad when he saw Lillian's face. "Sorry, Mom. I just wanted to see the old neighborhood." He punched the glove with the ball.

Lillian put her hands on his shoulders. "Promise me you'll never to do that again," she said, her voice quivering.

"Don't worry. I won't." Tommy hoped she wasn't going to start crying; that would make him a little kid again. An argument would be better than that. "But you should have told me. I'm old enough. Right, Mr. Drooms?"

Drooms suddenly felt guilty when Lillian turned to him. He remained silent.

Lillian had the odd feeling that she was outnumbered. She stood up straight, and tried to sound cheerful. "I made spaghetti. Are you hungry?"

"Starving," said Tommy.

"Good. Go wash up."

Tommy headed off to the bathroom with Gabriel on his heels. Tommy grinned and tapped Gabriel's head with the glove. "Don't worry, Gabe. Mr. Drooms got one for you, too." He pulled a smaller glove from inside his jacket. "Here. See if it fits."

Gabriel put on the glove and ran to hug Mr. Drooms, and then ran back to Tommy and bombarded him with questions about the train, Saporito's, the ice cream.

Drooms had been smiling at Tommy, with a look of something like pride in his eyes. Lillian still felt sick to her stomach with fear that Tommy had been lost and guilt that it had been her fault, and now she felt anger at Tommy's apparent shift in allegiance. Drooms's easy smile set her off. "You bought him a baseball glove?"

Drooms was caught unawares. "I saw no harm in consoling the boy."

"Consoling him is my job."

Drooms opened his mouth and was about to speak. Instead he just nodded, and turned to leave.

Lillian immediately regretted taking out her fear and anger on him. "Mr. Drooms!" But her voice came out sounding like a command.

Drooms stopped, wondering what was coming next.

Lillian twisted her hands as she searched for the right tone. "Thank you for your help." No, that still sounded angry. In a gentler voice, she asked, "Won't you join us for dinner, please?"

"I think not. Goodnight, Mrs. Hapsey."

As she watched him leave and close the door behind him, a new wave of sadness washed over her.

Tommy came out and looked around. "Where's Mr. Drooms?"

"He had to go. He said he'll see you later."

Tommy gave a groan of disappointment and was almost ready to blame her again. He was sure that Mr. Drooms would want to stay to tell her all about Brooklyn. Then he saw that her eyes were wet from crying, but that she was trying to hide it.

"I'm sorry, Mom. I know that was wrong. Next time we'll go together." He hugged her and let her hug him back as she wiped her eyes again. When she stopped her silent crying, he sniffed the air. "Can we eat? That smells delicious."

All through dinner Lillian kept looking at Tommy, marveling at how quickly he moved from having an adult sensibility at times, to being just a little boy. She felt that he was slowly leaving her grasp. Throughout the meal, everything was "Mr. Drooms said…, Mr. Drooms knows…," increasing the distance she felt. Tommy was moving into a man's world, before her very eyes. He seemed so happy, as if the day had changed him and increased his confidence. Mr. Drooms had managed to connect him to the outside world in a way that she couldn't.

She sat quietly and let Tommy talk, even encouraged him, while she carefully memorized the details of her little boy as a nine-year-old – the way he talked excitedly with his hands, the sprinkle of tiny freckles across his nose, the way his mouth curled up in a half-smile when he told Gabriel about Mary, the soft roundness of his cheeks and chin that would soon be gone – carefully memorized these details, before they were left behind to childhood.

Later that night, after the boys had taken their baths and gone to bed, Lillian sat on her couch and stared into the fire. Now that she had recovered from the frenzy of the day, and had put away her worry and fear, now that Tommy was safe in his bed, only now did she allow herself to think of Mr. Drooms. She remembered the look of happiness on his face when he brought Tommy home, and how quickly she had dashed that happiness – trying to blame him for something that was her fault.

On the coffee table, her sketch pad was open to the picture of the frozen Drooms. She leaned over the sketch and ran her fingers across the drawing of him, gazing at him lovingly. Then she reached under the couch and pulled out a thin box and placed it on her lap. She slipped off the red ribbon, opened the box, and lifted a burgundy scarf to her cheek. She had impulsively bought it for Mr. Drooms while she was at the department stores. But she doubted she would have the courage to give it to him, especially after today. She put it back and slid the box under the couch.

She glanced over at the bookshelves, at the photograph of her and Tom on their wedding day. Tom was a sweetness from long ago that she would always cherish. But she was no longer that girl in the photo. So much had changed since then. Long, lonely years had passed, during which she had struggled and survived and made a new life for herself. She was stronger, more sure of who she was, and what she wanted from life.

She gazed into the dying fire. The burned-down logs released a soft crackling and snapping sound. For a few hypnotic moments, she watched as they changed from red to gray, from fire to ash.

Then she stood, reached for the poker, and stirred the embers into flame, feeling the increased heat as she shifted the logs. She stood near the rekindled fire and allowed the heat to warm her.

She sat back on the couch and held up the drawing of Drooms in the snow. She tried to imagine him in spring or summer, without his coat and hat, with a light breeze blowing his hair – and found that she could not. He seemed a man made for winter, born of winter – stiff, hunched, dressed in charcoal gray, like a cold chunk of charcoal that had never known flame. No wonder he was so cold.

She took a pencil and put the pad on her lap. She started to sketch a female figure next to him – in a long robe and flowing hair. The woman held a flame in her cupped hands, offering warmth to the frozen man.

Lillian held the drawing at a distance, and then placed it on her lap again. She animated the female figure by adding folds and curves to her robe; then she drew a few more flickering petals of flames. She looked at the couple, then closed the sketch pad, and held it to her breast.

Chapter 10

∾

Drooms left work late, and walked a few blocks out of his way in order to pass by Gimbels. He wanted to see the place where Mason worked, though he had no intention of going inside.

He had thought a lot about Mason lately, and for the life of him, he couldn't reconstruct the chain of thoughts that had led him to believe that Mason was leaving him. Drooms knew him to be an honorable, trustworthy man – even considered him a friend. Though Drooms often used work as an excuse to lunch with Mason, the truth was he enjoyed his company. In all their years together, Drooms could remember nothing but kind words, encouragement, and a sense of humor in the most trying times. Mason certainly deserved better than what he had gotten all these years working for him. Far better.

Drooms had to thread his way around the mothers and fathers with their children lined up to look at the window decorations, people listening to the carolers and street musicians on the corners, shoppers weighted down by bags, couples with their arms linked.

In front of Gimbels people jostled to get a better view of the window displays. Drooms stood at the back of the crowd, but over their heads, he could see a Christmas tree, heavy with tinsel and colored ornaments, set in the center of a recreated living room. At the tree's base nestled a miniature snowy village with an electric train running around the shops, the church, the tiny houses. Next to the tree a mannequin family gathered around the family hearth, and stockings hung from the mantel.

In the crowd near the window, Drooms saw what he took to be a mother and daughter, pointing to the wife mannequin who sat in an armchair, wearing a long green satin robe trimmed with white lace. The daughter squeezed her mother's arm and leaned her head dreamily on her mother's shoulder. So like his sister Kate at that age. He thought of the unopened Christmas card in his desk.

The sound of knocking on the glass caused Drooms to look at the adjacent window where an employee was adding to the toys and games display. When the employee turned around, Drooms realized with a start that it was Mason, and he stepped farther back behind the crowd. A few of the children pointed and tapped on the window, perhaps taking Mason for one of Santa's helpers.

Mason obliged the children by holding up a game of Parcheesi, a tube of Tinkertoys, a doll in a purple velvet dress.

Drooms smiled. There was his trusted colleague of so many years, apparently enjoying work that another man might object to. But then Mason was a different kind of man, who would do anything for his family – and do so with as much enjoyment possible. Yes, Mason was a remarkable man, in his quiet, unassuming way.

*

That evening, Lillian hung up the phone, and paced her living room, indecisive about what to do. Mrs. Kuntzman called saying she didn't feel well and Lillian had told her she would be right over. But Gabriel had a slight cold and she didn't want to bring him outside – but she didn't want to leave the boys alone either. She was torn between asking Mr. Drooms to look in on the boys, and leaving them alone.

Lillian regretted her unkind treatment of Mr. Drooms when he brought Tommy back from Brooklyn; but even more she regretted that she had needed his help. She hated to ask anyone for anything, and liked to think that she was strong and in control. Now here it was, only two days later, and she needed his help again.

She glanced over at Tommy and Gabriel, who were in their pajamas, coloring at the kitchen table. They would be fine. Tommy could always go to Mr. Drooms if he needed anything. But what if he wasn't even at home?

Drooms heard a knocking at his door, and with his pencil and papers still in his hand, he opened it and saw Lillian standing there. He wondered at the beating of his heart. But he quickly became concerned when he saw the hot water bottle in her hand, and glanced down the hall to where her apartment door stood open.

"Mrs. Hapsey, is everything all right?"

"I'm sorry to bother you. The boys are fine. It's Mrs. Kuntzman. She's feeling poorly and asked if I could stop by. She already called her daughter, but it could take a while for her to get here. I want to sit with her until she arrives." She looked down, then asked, "Would you mind just looking in on the boys? Gabriel has the sniffles and I don't want to bring him out in the night air."

"Of course. I'll sit with them, if you like. I won't leave until you get back."

This was more than she had expected. The worry left her face and her brow became smooth again. "They've had their dinner and bath. They won't need anything."

Drooms saw that the boys were now peeking around their doorway. He smiled and put his hand on Lillian's shoulder, reassuring her, and was immensely gratified by the small gesture of her leaning in towards his hand. For one moment, he thought she might rest her cheek on his hand.

"Don't worry," he said. "We'll be fine. Just a moment." He stepped inside, put his papers down, and then came back out and closed the door behind him.

Lillian walked back to Tommy and Gabriel and kissed them quickly on their cheeks. "Be good, boys. I'll be back soon." She placed her hand on Drooms's arm. "Thank you," she said, and then hurried down the stairs.

"Hi, Mr. Drooms," said Tommy. "We're off the whole week for Christmas – no school. So we get to stay up late."

Gabriel led Drooms to the kitchen table and showed him their work. "We're making pirate maps. Look."

Drooms leaned over each of their drawings, murmuring praise, and then took a seat at the table. He became aware of the intimacy at being in Lillian's home, sitting where she would sit, spending the evening in the way she would. It felt terribly personal.

He glanced over the apartment, noting where she had left a book near the couch, the holiday decorations, the hallway that led to her bedroom. He wondered what her bedroom was like, and then felt his face heat up, feeling like an interloper in her home.

When he returned his gaze to the table he saw that Gabriel was studying him. "What is it, Gabriel?"

"Billy said you used to be a pirate. He saw the skull and bones tattoo on your arm."

Tommy groaned and rolled his eyes. "Don't be a dope, Gabe. Pirates are from the olden days." He shook his head, and continued with his drawing.

But Gabriel persisted. "Well, were you a pirate?"

Drooms had to chuckle. "Not a pirate. But a sailor. I was in the Navy." He rolled up his sleeve past his elbow and showed them the tattoo of the anchor he had always regretted getting.

"I knew it!" said Gabriel. "Did you find any treasure?"

"No," laughed Drooms. "No treasure. But I saw some interesting places. A long time ago."

"In the olden days?" asked Gabriel.

Tommy groaned again. "He's not *that* old."

Drooms wondered if he really did look old. He had never minded when the neighborhood children called him Old Man, but now he worried that he had perhaps become the thing he had only pretended to be. He sat up a little straighter in the chair.

Tommy got up and went to the cookie jar on the counter. "Mommy lets us have cookies on special nights. Do you want some, Mr. Drooms?"

Drooms smiled. "No thanks, Tommy."

Gabriel looked up from his map. "Well, I do. And some milk."

"I know you do. Here." Tommy gave Gabriel a few cookies, and poured him a glass of milk. He then gave a cookie to Mr. Drooms. "Try one. Mom made them – chocolate chip."

Drooms took the cookie and bit into it, nodding that it was good. They sat quietly for a few moments, Gabriel humming to the Christmas songs on the radio. He lifted his head and asked Drooms, "What's figgy pudding?"

"I'm not really sure. I think it's some kind of..." He let his voice trail off, failing to come up with a reasonable explanation.

Suddenly Gabriel's face lit up. "Hey! I know. How about you tell us a story?"

Drooms shifted in his chair, disconcerted by this simple suggestion. "Oh. I don't know any stories."

Tommy put some more cookies on a plate and set them in the middle of the table. "That's okay, you can just make one up." He folded his legs under him on the chair, and bit into a cookie.

"I'm afraid that's something I'm not very good at," said Drooms.

But Tommy pushed on. "It's easy – Mommy showed us how. Watch. You go like this."

He pointed to Gabriel who began the story as he continued to color.

"Once upon a time…" He pointed to Tommy.

"There was a boy who…" Tommy pointed to Drooms.

Drooms looked from Tommy to Gabriel. Their heads popped up when they didn't hear anything. They waited for him to continue the story.

"Who – wanted to play," Drooms finally said.

Gabriel smiled now that Drooms had gotten the hang of it. He whispered, "Now you have to point to me."

Drooms pointed to him. Gabriel opened his eyes wide and continued. "Then one day, he was walking in the deeeep, daaaark forest. And…" He pointed to Tommy.

"And it was starting to get dark with thunder and lightning." Tommy imitated the booming and crashing of a storm. "When all of a sudden…" He pointed to Drooms.

Drooms was at a complete loss as to what happened next. He turned to Tommy and then to Gabriel, then back to Tommy. He opened his mouth and stuttered, "and then…and then…" He blinked at the kitchen table, waiting for something to come to his mind, but all he saw was a wide blank page stretching out before him. He stared at the whiteness of the empty page, overwhelmed that he didn't know. Such a simple thing, and he didn't know. Again he looked from one boy to the other. "I – I don't know what happens." Drooms felt himself sinking under the perplexity on their faces. "Why don't you two finish it?"

Tommy resumed his mapmaking. "Nah, it doesn't work very good with just two people. We already tried that."

They sat quietly, Drooms feeling that he had disappointed the boys. He had a sense of being on unfirm ground, of not recognizing familiar territory.

Tommy rummaged through the crayon box, and then hit on another idea. "We could read pirate books."

Gabriel sat up in his seat, his eyes wide with hope. "Will you read to us?"

Drooms nodded, relieved to have a task he was capable of performing. "We could do that."

Gabriel stuffed the rest of the cookie in his mouth, jumped up and ran to the living room. "Over here, Mr. Drooms. In the libary," he said, pulling a few books from the coffee table.

Tommy laughed. "He means the couch. That's where Mommy always reads to us." He walked with Drooms to the couch. "Here. You have to sit in the middle so we can see the pictures."

Drooms positioned himself in the middle of the couch. Gabriel sat next to him, then jumped up and ran to his bedroom. "Wait! I have to get my patch."

Drooms heard the sounds of drawers being opened and closed, a closet door sliding open, a bumping and tossing of objects.

"And my hook!" Gabriel called out.

Tommy took an umbrella from the stand near the door and peg-legged it to the hallway. "Yaargh, Blackbeard!" he called out in a pirate voice. "Hurry up! You're taking too long!"

Gabriel reappeared, fumbling with his eye patch and a hanger hook that protruded from his pajama sleeve.

"No, I'm Cap'n Hook," he whispered. Brandishing his hook, he called out in a raspy pirate voice, "Ahoy, maties!" He jumped on the couch next to Drooms. "You can be Blackbeard," he said, pointing to Drooms's shadowy cheek.

"Blackbeard," Drooms smiled. "Well. Here we are then."

The boys curled up and leaned over the book he held, just like they did with Lillian. Drooms was stiff at first, but little by little he got into the reading, and at the boys' insistence he read in the voices of pirates, scallywags, and shipwrecked sailors. The stories had obviously been read many times, and at certain passages they joined in a refrain, or pointed out a detail to Drooms in the illustrations.

As Drooms read the stories, he realized that he hadn't felt such connection in a long, long time and marveled that it should come from such a simple act. The boys took such pleasure in the stories, had such ready access to the world of adventure and make-believe.

Or, he wondered, did he feel such connection because they were *her* children, in *her* home?

After an hour and a half, the boys were starting to nod and close their eyes. Gabriel was the first to drop off to sleep, leaning against Drooms, his hook and patch abandoned to the floor.

Eventually Tommy also fell asleep, with half of the afghan pulled over him, the other half still over the back of the couch.

Drooms didn't want to wake the boys, so he sat silent and unmoving – though he did finish the last chapter to find out if the long-buried gold was ever discovered.

He looked around, noticing the tiny touches that made the apartment feel so different from his – the feminine bits of embroidery, the lace in the windows, framed family photographs, the boys' drawings on the shelves by the fireplace.

As he leaned his head back against the afghan, he caught a faint scent of what he guessed was her perfume or bath oil – was it lilac, roses? He closed his eyes and luxuriated in the warmth and comfort of her home.

From some deep, peaceful place he heard a noise that caught his attention, and to his surprise, he realized that he had fallen asleep. He rubbed his face, unsure if minutes or hours had passed. He heard the key turn in the lock, and saw Lillian gently opening the door.

When she saw Drooms, sunk in the middle of the couch with the boys sprawled all over, she couldn't keep from laughing. "Mr. Drooms. I'm sorry it took so long. Is everything all right?"

"Fine, fine." He hoped he didn't look like he had just woken up. It was highly unlike him. He never took naps or dozed off in the evenings.

He watched her take off her coat and hat and hang them on the hall tree. She had such a graceful, light way of moving.

Lillian came to the couch and helped extricate Drooms from the boys, shaking her head at the number of books they had piled up around them. Tommy woke up and walked sleepily to bed, as if it were a night like any other.

"Night, Mommy. Night, Mr. Drooms."

Lillian carried Gabriel to bed and tucked him in. When she came out she saw that Drooms was gathering the scattered books and stacking them on the coffee table.

"How is Mrs. Kuntzman feeling?"

Lillian sat on the arm of the couch. "She's resting now. It's her rheumatism acting up. Her daughter will stay a few days. I didn't want her to be alone."

"No, of course not. You did the right thing."

Lillian glanced down and played with the button on her sweater. "Mr. Drooms, I owe you an apology for the other day, when you brought Tommy home."

"No, you don't," he said, shaking his head. "You were worried. I completely understand."

"No. What I said was wrong." She was silent a few moments, and then looked up. "I didn't want you to think I was a bad mother."

Drooms let his mouth fall open, shocked to hear this, and even more surprised that it mattered to her what he thought. "Not at all – on the contrary." He was about to say he couldn't imagine a more perfect mother, but instead said, "Perhaps I was out of line."

"No, you weren't. I can't thank you enough for what you did. I don't know what you said to Tommy but he's been different ever since." Lillian threw her hands open. "And now I'm in your debt again."

Drooms waved this away.

"Is this what happens when you get old?" Lillian asked. "You start needing more help?"

Drooms smiled. "Are you asking me as the aged expert?"

She laughed and stood, shaking her head and reaching for the afghan. Drooms took the other end and helped her with it, their hands touching briefly for the final fold. Lillian placed the afghan over the back of the couch. "I hope they weren't too much trouble."

"None at all. And I've learned quite a bit about pirates tonight. I was Blackbeard." He rubbed his cheek in explanation.

Lillian laughed at the idea. "And did you read in character?"

"Yes. After some initial instruction."

She laughed again, and wondered at her high spirits. It seemed that everything was fine once more, that life was happy, exciting, promising.

"Mr. Drooms. What would you say to a glass of my hot buttered rum?"

Drooms gave it a thought, and nodded. "I would say that's a drink worthy of a pirate."

She gestured towards the kitchen table. "Please. Have a seat. It will just take a minute."

She heated a pan of water and added the butter, rum, and brown sugar. Then she rummaged through the cupboard and took out the vanilla and spices, adding the ingredients as she listened to Drooms.

He told her about the stories he had read to the boys, and how Gabriel had jumped up at certain parts to enact the scene.

Lillian watched him as he leaned back in the chair, his face so mobile, so relaxed. She realized she was seeing a side of him that most people must not know about. She found herself talking easily to him as she prepared the drinks, as if she had known him for long years.

"They've been in a pirate stage ever since Tommy read *Treasure Island*," she said, pouring the drinks. "Everything is buried treasures and secret maps." She placed a steaming mug in front of Drooms and took her seat.

"I seem to remember a similar stage myself," said Drooms. "I guess it's something boys are drawn to. Going off, exploring the world, having adventures."

Lillian raised her glass mug. "To the Seven Seas!"

"Hear, hear." Drooms clinked his mug to hers and took a sip. He inhaled the fragrant drink and looked at the mug. "Very nice. I haven't had a glass of this – in years." After a moment, he smiled and took another sip. "It might help to melt off some of those icicles."

Lillian put her head in her hands and laughed. "Oh, that was just an impulse. That night I saw you standing out in the snow. I didn't mean anything by it."

"I guess I can be a little cold at times."

"A little? It took me two weeks to get the courage to say hello to you."

Drooms smiled. "I don't usually open up to people. A fault of mine."

"Ah, well. We all have faults. Though I almost gave up that day you snatched back your package from me."

Drooms chuckled, remembering his actions. "Well, I'm glad you didn't."

His words caused them to sit quietly for a few moments.

Then Drooms looked around and gestured to the Christmas decorations. "You've made it quite festive."

Lillian followed his gaze to the Christmas tree and stockings, the paper chains around the door frame, the snowflakes hanging in the windows.

"It means a lot to the boys. We don't have family around here so I try to make it special for them."

She was hoping her comment might spur Drooms to say something about his own family, but he remained silent. From the day she first saw him she had wondered if he'd ever been married or involved with anyone. She assumed he had always been a bachelor, but couldn't be sure. She spoke casually before taking a sip from her mug.

"Do – do you have family?"

Drooms leaned back in his chair. "None of my own. I never married."

Lillian blushed to find that he had interpreted her question so accurately.

Drooms never spoke to anyone about his past, but he felt that he wanted her to know something of him.

"I have family in the Midwest – but I've lost touch with them."

"What a shame. Is there no contact at all?"

"Oh, cards at Christmas. That sort of thing."

Lillian felt sad to think that he was without family – she could hardly imagine it. "I miss my family terribly. My sister and her family live upstate so we don't get to see each other very often. And Tom didn't have much family, an aunt and uncle, a few cousins. It's so nice to have family around – especially for the holidays."

She waited for him to respond but he simply smiled and looked over at the tree. Then she too examined the tree, with only a few presents under it. She thought of all the holiday preparations she still needed to do, and gave a deep sigh.

"I so wanted this Christmas to be special, but I find that I'm falling short. The tree wouldn't even be up if it weren't for you. And it needs a new top ornament. I still have gifts to wrap, and I've barely started my Christmas baking." In a softer voice she added, "And now I seem to have a way of intruding on your evenings."

Drooms leaned forward and took her hand. "Not at all. Not at all."

He didn't want her to feel bad about asking for his help, and the gesture to reach out to her had been completely spontaneous. But now that her warm hand was in his, he felt that some wall had finally crumbled between them. That simple, gentle touch was like the click of a key, finally unlocking a door.

They held each other's gaze, and slowly leaned in – Drooms surprised to find himself so easily following his heart, Lillian astonished that she felt such passion for him. She realized that she had wanted to hold him from that first moment on the stairs.

"Mommy, I'm cold," came Gabriel's sleepy voice from his bedroom.

They smiled and reluctantly sat back. Lillian looked down at their linked hands, and then stood up. "I'll get another blanket for him."

Drooms ran his hand through his hair and cleared his throat as he waited for her to return. He felt exposed, as if his protective facade had fallen away. It was a new feeling, and he wasn't sure if he liked being so vulnerable. But when he saw her come back, with that smile of hers, he knew that he was going to throw all caution to the wind.

But the few moments with Gabriel had caused Lillian to pull back a little, to doubt herself – she didn't always trust her highs and lows. Perhaps she was just seeing and hearing what she wanted. She would slow things down, try to see them clearly.

"Gabriel's fine now. I think he was dreaming." She stood by the table and gestured towards his mug. "A warm-up?"

Drooms lifted his glass. "Please."

She went to the stove, and refilled their mugs.

He leaned back in his chair, seeming to understand her quietness. All he wanted was to be in her presence, to know her, listen to her. He asked her about her days in Brooklyn, and then about her youth.

They soon fell right back into easy conversation, and for the next hour they sat comfortably, speaking freely of their lives. She described the various art classes she had taken, and her girlish dreams of studying in Paris. He spoke of his years in the Navy, of the places he had seen, and how he had settled in New York after the war. He recounted how he had built his business from a one-man show, to now having a staff of twelve. She told him of her years in the department store, and now at the switchboard, and how she was going to brush up on her typing to get a better job, and perhaps try to get into the Art Department.

"Yes, you really must get a portfolio together and take it around. There's a quality to your work that is immediate, and stirring –"

The clock from the mantel began to strike, seeming to go on forever, marking the lateness of the evening, and intruding on the intimacy of their conversation. A few moments of silence sat between them.

Drooms spoke first. "Well. It's getting late for you." He pushed back his chair.

"Yes, I suppose it is," said Lillian.

They stood and slowly walked to the door. Drooms rested his hand on the doorknob and turned to look at her. "Well."

"Well, thank you again for sitting with the boys. Blackbeard."

Drooms smiled. "Thanks for the rum. Matey." He stood before her and beheld her face, wanting to take every detail with him: her smile with the tiniest suggestion of a dimple, the way her curls brushed against her shoulders, but most of all, the softness in her eyes.

"Goodnight, Mr. Drooms." Lillian wanted to ask if he would stop by again tomorrow, and if not, then the next day and the next. But instead she simply smiled.

Drooms opened the door, and hesitated before saying, "You can call me Charles, if you like."

"Charles," Lillian said slowly, taking possession of his name, as if cradling it in her hands. "And you can call me Lillian."

"Lillian." Of course she would have such a lovely name. "Well, goodnight, Lillian." He wanted to say it again and again.

The door closed between them.

They knew that having each other's name brought them closer, was something they were taking with them that they didn't have at the beginning of the evening. But they didn't know that after saying goodnight, they both stood staring at the door between them, wanting what was on the other side.

Lillian reached for the doorknob, then refrained. Drooms was about to knock, but pulled his hand back.

He remembered her sweet, low tones that soothed and caressed. Lillian thought of the warmth of his hand in hers.

She took a step away, paused, and then turned back to the door. Drooms placed his hand on the door, then once again changed his mind.

Thirty seconds of mirrored desire and indecision passed between them.

Then just as Drooms decided to knock, Lillian opened the door. They held each other's gaze, took a step towards each other, and embraced, sinking into the warmth of one another – layers and layers of a fit so perfect they could almost hear the click, click, click of a myriad tiny gears and locks finding and settling into place.

"Mommy, I wet the bed. It's cold," came Gabriel's voice again.

They slowly separated and looked into each other's eyes. But it was all right. Something had already been sealed, confirmed, acknowledged. Nothing else mattered.

Drooms put his hand on her cheek, and she covered it with her hand. They leaned into a long, slow kiss. When they separated, it was as though they were still embraced, still warm and full of each other.

"Goodnight, Charles." A sweet wave of tenderness washed over Lillian, and the future spread before her like a beautiful land.

"Goodnight. Lillian." Drooms left knowing that his life had changed.

Chapter 11

The following afternoon Lillian was in the middle of her Christmas baking. She wore her ruffled red and green Christmas apron and bustled about the kitchen, singing along with the radio. She didn't want to appear too different to the boys, but she couldn't forget that kiss, the warm embrace. She kept catching herself smiling as she remembered his hand in her hair, the gentleness in his voice when he said her name.

When Al Bowlly's "Only Forever" came on, she turned up the volume and tried to dance with the boys. She could usually count on at least Gabriel to play along, but today both boys were restless and wanted to go outside, and the more she laughed and tried to twirl around with them, the more impatient they became.

"Can't we go now, Mom?" asked Tommy. "I already read all my books, and if we don't go now the library will close."

"Yeah, Mommy, I want to go outside. I need some more books, too." Gabriel ran to get his coat and started to put it on.

Lillian opened the oven, took out a batch of Christmas cookies, and set them on top of the stove.

"If we can't go today," she said, "we'll go another day."

"But I already read –"

"Now Tommy, what did I say? I can't leave in the middle of baking."

Gabriel stomped his foot. "But Mommy –"

"If you two don't start behaving I won't take you to see Santa tomorrow."

Gabriel gasped at this possibility. "Mommy, we have to see Santa to tell him what we want!"

Tommy heard Drooms's door open and close, and ran to look down the hall.

"Hi, Mr. Drooms!"

Gabriel also ran to the door and peeked out.

"Hi, Mr. Drooms! Will you take us to the libary?"

Drooms appeared in their doorway, dressed to go outside. He smiled at the boys, then at Lillian.

But she didn't want to cross any as yet to be determined boundary. "Boys! Stop that. You know better." She went to the door, pulled the boys back inside, and widened her eyes at them in warning.

Tommy relented. "Okay, okay."

Lillian flushed with pleasure as she gazed up at Drooms. She had never seen him looking so handsome.

"Hello, Lillian."

"Hello. Charles."

Tommy and Gabriel jerked back their heads, and pronounced the name in one long, upturned question. "Charles?"

Drooms covered Lillian's embarrassment by inhaling a whiff of her cooking. "Something smells mighty good."

"Just doing some baking. You're home early today?"

Drooms was about to explain, but Gabriel stomped again, impatient with all this talking.

"I want to go outside!"

Lillian was about to reprimand him but Drooms spoke up. "I'm going out anyway to run a few errands. I don't mind. And it looks like you could use some time alone."

She didn't want to give in, but Drooms pressed his point. "They just have a touch of cabin fever. A little fresh air will do them good."

Gabriel let his whole body droop and put a hand to his head. "Please, Mommy, please? I have a cabin fever."

Tommy raised his eyebrows in hope.

Lillian cast a side glance to Drooms who gave her a reassuring nod.

"All right. But you boys are not to waylay Mr. Drooms like that. Do you understand?"

"Yippee!" Gabriel held Drooms's hand and smiled up at him.

"Anything you say, Mom!" Tommy ran to get his coat.

Lillian buttoned Gabriel's coat and pulled his mittens over his hands.

Tommy dashed past them and stood outside in the hall. "Come on! Bye, Mom."

Drooms and Lillian gazed at one another before they left. Lillian was filled with a happiness she hadn't known in a long time; Drooms felt as if some heavy, stiff garment had finally fallen from him, and he was now light and mobile.

Lillian called after them as she closed the door: "You two mind Charles, now!"

Drooms froze and stared back at the closed door, his mouth open in surprise. She used the very words. Why did she have to say that? He felt his heart beating high in his chest, and he felt all prickly with dread as he recalled those exact words from his mother, calling after him – the last time he ever saw her happy: "You two mind Charles, now!" And the twins, Sarah and Sam, holding his hands as they left for the woods to find their tree.

Drooms stood rooted to the floor, stunned to find himself in the same scenario, the very situation he had so carefully avoided all these years. Here he was again, in charge of two little lives. What had he been thinking? He knew not to open himself up like this. He knew, and yet he had let it happen. A dark foreboding spread through him, crowding out the buoyant feelings of just a moment ago. He didn't want to go on, but the boys pulled on his arms.

Gabriel led the way down the stairs.

"C'mon, Mr. Drooms!"

"Hurry, Mr. Drooms, the library's gonna close!" said Tommy.

Drooms tried to shake off the feeling, telling himself that he was overreacting. He followed the boys down the stairs, but images from the past began to bubble up.

When Tommy opened the vestibule door, Drooms saw that it was snowing softly. He took firm hold of the boys' hands. "I want you to hold my hand tightly when we're outside. It might be slippery."

Tommy thought he was a little old for this, but he didn't care, as long as they were outside. While they walked the boys chatted non-stop about snow forts and presents and Santa.

But Drooms became increasingly distracted as memories began to string themselves together from that day in 1907. Tommy and Gabriel had the same bubbly excitement that the twins had on setting out to find their Christmas tree. The snow that day glistened in the sun from a sky that was pure, innocent blue. The scent of wood fire from the nearby farms added a hint of warmth to the cold, clear air. Once again, he heard the crunching of his boots as he traipsed through the snow, could feel the tiny resistance of the newly crusted snow as his boot broke through with each step. It was a perfect winter day.

"Look Charlie, the snow is full of sparkles," said Sarah, as she let the glittering snow fall through her fingers.

Sam had scooped up a bunch of snow and tossed it into the air. Then he threw a handful at Sarah, "Have some sparkles!"

She chased him down and threw handfuls of snow at him. They were like playful puppies, throwing snow and giggling as they tumbled over each other.

Drooms tried to stop the memories, push them back, away from him. He tried to focus on what Tommy and Gabriel were saying, but when they passed The Red String Curio Store, the boys stopped and stared at the window display.

The day was conspiring against him, for there in the window was a set of women's hair combs, so like the ones he had bought that Christmas for his sweetheart, Rachel. He had wrapped them in green print paper. Under the combs he had placed a poem for her – "sweet face, hair like lace, eyes of blue, heart so true" – his imperfect attempt to tell her how he felt about her.

Tommy and Gabriel broke free and ran to the window on the other side to look at the toys displayed for Christmas.

The longer Drooms gazed at the hair combs, the fresher that day in 1907 became. His body dizzily flooded with memory, his vision swirled and swerved and once again Rachel was before him, with her brother Caleb. They were just turning into their farm lane and stopped to talk.

"We're gonna find our tree!" Sam hollered out to them.

Sarah held up her red ribbon to show to Rachel. "And I'm going to tie this around it so Charlie can find it again."

Caleb smiled at the twins. "We got our tree yesterday. Out behind the pond."

"Oh, it's beautiful Charlie," said Rachel. "Why don't you come by and see it? You can help trim it."

"Yeah, Charlie, stop on by," Caleb said as he started down the lane.

The twins giggled and ran past Rachel and Charlie.

Rachel's cheeks were rosy from the cold, her eyes smiling with merriment. She kept turning her head to keep her long hair from blowing in her face. Then she burst into that laughter of hers as she watched Sam and Sarah leapfrog and tumble in the snow as they ran down the path into the woods.

Rachel took a step towards Charlie and twisted her shoulders from side to side, suddenly bashful. "Come by the house, Charlie. We made that spice bread you like so much. Mother calls it 'Charlie's bread.'"

"Well, I can't pass up that, can I? Besides, I have something for you – for under the tree."

"You do? For me? Oh, give me a hint."

Charlie smiled, and looking at her long dark tresses, he moved a strand of hair that had blown across her face.

Rachel's eyes grew bright as she guessed that the gift was something for her hair.

Charlie glanced up and down the path, and not seeing Caleb or the twins, he took her hand and gave her a quick kiss on the cheek. Rachel smiled and took his other hand. For a few brief seconds, life surrounded them in its sweetness: Charlie imagined them walking hand in hand through the woods, visiting each other's farms, bringing each other little tokens of affection, and someday courting. The late afternoon sun cast a golden aura around Rachel's hair and Charlie knew he had made the right decision in the red enameled combs. It was a moment of perfection. Time stood still. And he was utterly happy.

Until that moment was shattered by screams.

"Charlie!" a terrified scream. Was it Sarah or Sam?

"Charlie! Charlie!" came cries of desperation. "Help us!"

Charlie's legs buckled beneath him. "Get Caleb!" he yelled to Rachel as he tore down the path.

His stomach twisted and lurched. He ran and followed the screams, calling out, "Sam! Sarah!"

His legs were not moving fast enough.

"Charlie! Help!" The screams were coming from near the pond. "Charlie!"

Fear flooded his face and he ran down the path, thinking No, no, no.

The tree branches lashed his face and every root and rock rose up from the path and caused him to trip and stumble, losing precious seconds. Almost to the pond. He would get there in time.

Then the cries stopped. A terrifying silence. His own screams became louder and more frantic, as if his voice were a rope that could reach them, help them to hold on. "Sam! Sarah!"

The rough the bare trees he saw that the twins had gone out on the frozen pond. They stood terrified with their arms held out as the ice was cracking, giving way beneath them.

Then, in desperation, they lurched towards each other and clung together tightly, causing the ice to give way, just as Charlie reached the pond.

In horror he watched as they fell through, grabbing at the ice and each other.

"Hold on! Hold on!" He started to run out on the ice, but Caleb now ran up, and held him back.

The rest was always a blur – where the branch had come from that he used to shimmy out to the hole in the ice; frantically grasping at an empty sleeve, an arm, a floating boot, a hand; crying for them to hold on, as he too began to fall through. Then, reaching and grasping and finally clenching his hands on each of their coats – his arms straining, trying and trying, but unable to lift them, the coats weighted with icy water. His mind told him to let go of one to save the other, but his hands would not obey. He couldn't abandon either of them to the lone, dark cold beneath the ice. He would not let go. He would go down with them, but he would not let go. He heard his voice, calling to them, begging them to hold on. On the ice, next to his face, his eyes fixed on the green mitten that lay on the snow, the curve of the little hand shape, so green against the white.

It seemed like years before Rachel and a farm hand arrived with the ladder; years before they were finally able to pull the little bodies out; years before they could pry his fingers loose from the coats, and stop his screaming.

Across the street from The Red String Curio Store, the neighbor boy Billy spotted Gabriel and hollered out to him.

"Hey, Gabriel! Look what I got!"

Gabriel spun around and gasped at the puppy Billy held up. Then both boys ran towards each other, just as a car rounded the corner and sped towards them. Billy and Gabriel both screamed out.

Tommy ran towards the screeching car, waving his arms, shouting, "Stop! Gabriel!"

The air suddenly filled with screams.

Drooms's face scrunched in perplexity as he stared at the combs in the window. He heard the children's screams. But they were not the voices of Sarah and Sam.

Drooms turned from the shop window, his stomach rolling. Gabriel was running into the street, in front of an oncoming car. Everyone was screaming.

He saw the car brake and skid. He heard choking sounds coming from his own mouth. He would get there in time, and yet he couldn't move; he was rooted to that icy pond, frozen, his words, his breath, nothing responding to his will. There was the same pounding heart, the same desperation of thought, willing it not to be true, willing to get there in time.

And yet he could not move. Everything rushed past him, the people running, the screams and voices swirling around him, car doors opening and slamming. He stood helpless between two worlds.

In horror, he saw Gabriel lying in the snow near the front bumper.

Drooms shook his head, no, no. It couldn't be.

Again. It had happened again. Again, his fault.

He couldn't breathe or blink or move his mind. He just stood there, slack-jawed, staring at the little body in the snow. He would have to carry it home again. He would have to face those screams from his mother and sister again when they saw what he carried in his arms, in Caleb's arms.

He saw Tommy running, then bending over his brother, a look of terror on his young face. Tommy knelt next to Gabriel, talking to him.

Drooms thought he was still crumpled at the pond, but another part of him was now kneeling next to Gabriel, though he didn't remember running across the snow and bending down. Drooms lifted Gabriel in his arms. This body was not icy cold, this body moved, and its eyes were weeping. Not dead? Not dead?

Drooms tried to pry apart the pond from the street. Tried to make sense of what was happening. He heard his own voice reaching him as if from far away. A man's voice, not a boy's. "Gabriel! Gabriel! Are you hurt?"

Gabriel softly cried. When he saw the crowd of people staring at him, he buried his face into Drooms's chest.

Tommy rubbed Gabriel's arm. "You're all right, Gabe. C'mon. You're okay." He turned to Drooms, as if to comfort him. "He just fell. He didn't get hit. I saw it. He's okay."

All around them, people were arguing, asking questions. Billy's father, the driver of the car, frightened passers-by. Drooms let their voices blur as he gently stood with Gabriel, holding him close, looking at his face, and then holding him close again.

The driver stood in the snow, clearly shaken, but seeing that Gabriel and Billy were all right, he yelled at Billy's father. "What, are you trying to give me a heart attack? Watch your kids!"

"You shouldn't be driving so fast! You almost hit them!"

The driver waved his words away, pushed through the onlookers, and drove off.

Drooms didn't fully trust what he saw. It seemed that Gabriel was all right, had not been hit. Or was he imagining it? Was he willing it to be true? Part of him still held the body of little Sam in his arms. He looked down again at Gabriel, half expecting him to be cold and blue. But Gabriel was alive.

Drooms turned to Tommy, he trusted Tommy. Tommy was speaking to Gabriel, and Gabriel was listening to him, nodding. Tommy must be right. Drooms looked again from Tommy to Gabriel and back to Tommy. Gabriel was alive. He had not been hurt.

Billy, still cradling the puppy, was lifted up by his father. They crossed over to Gabriel, who had his arms linked around Drooms's neck.

"You okay, Gabriel?" asked Billy's father. "Billy, what the heck were you thinking!" He patted Gabriel, "You okay, Gabe?" then back to Billy, "You know better than that. What have I told you a hundred times?"

"Stop-look-and-listen, but Daddy I wanted Gabriel to see my new puppy."

His father held Billy tight and kept kissing his head and apologizing to Drooms. "I knew I shouldn't have gotten the dog. Jeez, I'm so sorry. I never know what he's going to do. I swear he's shaving years off my life. You sure you're all right, Gabe? C'mon, Billy. Let's go home."

Drooms couldn't stop shaking; his whole body vibrated as if shivering from extreme cold, and yet he was drenched in sweat. With awkward, jarring movements and trembling hands, he smoothed Gabriel's hair and kissed his warm forehead.

"C'mon Gabe, you're okay," Tommy said, taking charge. "He's okay, Mr. Drooms. Billy always does stuff like that. You have to be more careful, Gabriel. C'mon, when we get home you can play with my Lincoln Logs."

As they set out for home, Tommy's words eventually took away Gabriel's fear. Gabriel wriggled down from Drooms's arms and wedged himself between Drooms and Tommy, holding their hands.

Drooms walked silently, staring straight ahead. He forced himself to be alert, to be on this sidewalk, in this city, now. He heard every word Tommy and Gabriel spoke.

And yet the long suppressed memories pushed their way up, forcing Drooms to look at them: there he was, standing at the burial, cruel flurries stinging his eyes. His mother's sobs ripping out his heart. His sister Kate, with her swollen, quivering face trying so hard to be strong. The black procession back to the farmhouse.

He had not cried that day, nor any day since. He remained alone at the graves, immobile, frozen, leaving only when darkness began to fall. Then, just beside the barn, like a little sign from the grave, their tiny rabbit lay outside his pen, barely moving in the snow. He placed it inside his jacket, determined to keep it alive. But failing, once again failing them.

The next day he had walked into town, to the grain and feed store, to the back counter. Under the deer head and the stuffed beaver and bobcat, he pulled out the tiny dead rabbit, and handed it to the taxidermist.

Happiness can hinge on a minute, he thought, on a second's miscalculated choice. On the desire to spend one more moment with your sweetheart, to see her smile at your words, to catch the sunlight in her hair. One tiny slip, and everything could change forever.

*

They arrived at Lillian's apartment, Tommy and Gabriel talking over one another as they recounted what happened.

Lillian lay Gabriel on the couch, covered him with the afghan, and kept smoothing back his hair. She looked from Tommy to Gabriel as she tried to piece together what had happened.

Drooms never took his eyes off Gabriel, except once, when he glanced at Lillian and saw the anguish in her face, her head in her hands. He imagined the gratitude she must feel at the near escape from another family tragedy.

Gabriel kicked off the cover saying he was hot, and sat up. Drooms saw that the boys were laughing, talking. They had all been spared.

He quietly left, dimly aware of a voice calling after him, "Mr. Drooms? Charles!"

He walked down the stairs and out of the building, wanting to be far, far away.

Lillian was surprised by Drooms's reaction. Did he think she blamed him? She knew only too well how quickly things could happen with the boys. Between the two of them there had been broken bones, stitches, a chipped tooth, nose bleeds…

"Mom, the car didn't hit him," said Tommy. "I saw it. It was all Billy's fault."

She wrapped her arms around Gabriel and kissed him. "You could have been hurt."

"No he wouldn't," said Tommy. "Gabriel knows better than to run out in the street, don't you Gabe?"

"Yeah, Mommy, I know better than that. I just wanted to see the puppy."

"How about some hot chocolate, Mom?" Tommy asked.

She smiled at his attempt to shift her focus. His tender protectiveness, the fright of the near accident, the flight of Drooms, brought her close to tears.

Gabriel's enthusiasm snapped her into action. "And some cookies? Can we, Mommy? It's a cozy day."

Lillian nodded and went to the kitchen to prepare their treat. She set a plate of cookies on the coffee table, glanced at the clock, and then turned on the radio.

"Look what time it is, boys. You're just in time for your show."

From the radio they heard, "Jack Armstrong – The Aaaaaaaaall American Boy." The boys snuggled together under the afghan, and munched and sipped as they listened to the sounds of a typhoon bashing a ship in a far-off sea. Tommy laughed at Gabriel's wide-eyed expressions.

Lillian started to prepare dinner. She washed and chopped the vegetables, alternating between feelings of relief that Gabriel was all right, anger that Drooms had left like that, and sadness at the look on his face. He just wasn't used to children, she thought. She could understand how he would be shaken, but she didn't like that she was now worried about him, too.

She made a fire for the boys and let them eat their dinners in front of it, their plates on the coffee table.

"This is just like camping," said Gabriel. "Hey! Can we sleep in front of our campfire tonight?"

"Not tonight, honey. I want you to get a good sleep. Maybe in a few days. Then we'll even roast marshmallows. How about that?"

"Can we go to camp this summer?" asked Tommy.

"Yeah, can we go to camp?" echoed Gabriel.

Lillian sighed. Always ten steps ahead of me, she thought, always racing into the future.

"We'll see." She ran her hands through Gabriel's hair, checking for any bumps or swelling, but he appeared to be fine.

While the boys listened to their radio shows, she washed the dishes, and thought about Drooms. Periodically she looked out the window for him, but saw only the falling snow under the streetlights.

*

After the fire died down, after the boys were asleep, she sat on the couch and waited for Drooms to return. Once or twice she thought she heard him coming up the stairs and glanced out her door. He just needs some time alone, she told herself. Yet inside, she felt a darkness growing, a fear that what happened today had changed everything.

*

Drooms kept his head down and his hands in his pockets as he walked in the snow, from street to street, farther and farther, not heeding where he was going. Just getting away from what almost happened. The cold was sealing him up again, freezing him into the past once more.

He pushed down all the happiness and hopes of yesterday, and exhausted himself by walking. The thought of Lillian, of their warm embrace, was only a dream now. As if it had never happened.

In spite of the dizzying dread and sickness that still filled him, he was grateful that the relationship had not developed. He was not cut out for it. He was better off alone. He had known that all these long years. And she will be much better off without me, he thought, as she must now realize.

*

Lillian stared at the dull glow from the dying fire, just a few faint glimmers behind the gray ashes. Now and then the embers would catch and flicker into life, and then die down and become even darker, as if from the effort. The longer she sat, the more she feared that it was over between her and Drooms, before it had even begun.

Sometime after midnight Lillian heard the vestibule door open, and heard his slow tread on the stairs. She shook off the afghan, opened her door, and stood in the hall waiting for him.

A shaft of sorrow pierced her as she saw him climb the last few stairs. He was covered in snow. His face, his whole bearing cold, frozen.

"Oh, Charles. Where were you all this time? Oh, you're frozen! Let me fix you something hot. Come inside."

She started to brush the snow off his coat but he moved away from her touch. She took a step back and tried to read his expression. "Gabriel's fine," she said. "He was just scared."

But her words had no effect. He stood expressionless, and then began to move away.

She grabbed his arm and spoke lightly. "They're always doing that to me. They're giving me gray hair." She brushed a hand to her head and tried to laugh.

When he still didn't respond, her expression changed to one of desperation. "Charles! Look at me!"

Drooms finally faced her and spoke softly. "I can't do it. I'm sorry." He began to walk towards his door.

Lillian followed him, not wanting to believe him. "Charles! Don't be ridiculous. It could just as easily have happened with me. It does happen with me, all the time."

"Please, leave me alone." He stiffly took the keys out of his pocket and began to open his door, his frozen fingers struggling to find the lock.

She grabbed his arm and forced him to look at her. "Charles!"

He turned on her harshly. "I don't want anything to do with you!"

Lillian took a step back as if he had slapped her cheek. She watched him step inside and close the door behind him. She heard the cold, metallic click of the lock. And then silence. She looked at the hardness of the door, knowing that it wouldn't open again. After a few stunned moments, she walked back to her apartment.

She closed her door, sat on the couch, and quietly wept. The darkness from the black pit reached up and slowly pulled her down.

*

Having walked for hours in the snow, Drooms was disoriented with fatigue and cold. He knew his words were cruel, but they were for her benefit, he believed. He shook off his coat, and pried his frozen feet out of his sodden shoes.

Then he saw the boy sitting quietly on the couch. Drooms clenched his hands, his jaw, furious.

The boy spoke in a soft voice. "That wasn't your fault."

"You! This is all *your* fault! I want you out of here, do you hear me? Out!"

The boy tried to squirm away but Drooms grabbed him roughly by the arm and pushed him towards the inner room.

"I just wanted to play," said the boy, wincing in fear.

"I want you out of my life – once and for all. Out! I never want to see you again! God help me. Never!"

The boy began to cry but Drooms was hardened to his tears and wrenched him to the inner room.

"Don't make me go back," pleaded the boy. "Please don't put me away. No, no!"

Drooms shoved him into the room, locked the door, and pounded on it. "Never come back! Never! Do you hear me? Never!"

He staggered backwards towards his bedroom and collapsed on his bed. Alone. He was utterly alone in the world except for the gnawing guilt and sorrow that would never leave him, his companions all these long years. He held his head in his hands and muttered confusedly. "I can't do it, I can't do it. I'm so sorry, Sam, Sarah, I'm so, so sorry."

In a state of fevered confusion, images swirled in his head of the twins laughing and playing, riding on his shoulders, giggling at the dinner table – then their frozen little bodies laid out in the parlor. Fitful images of his mother blurred into Lillian saying, "You two mind Charles, now." His mother's words, "I can always count on my Charles," blended into strangled screams. Confused memories of him as a happy little boy shifted to him standing frozen at the burial, then morphed into Tommy standing in the snow, then to Gabriel lying dead on the couch. The sad eyes of the little boy as he slammed the door on him, turned into the sad eyes of Lillian as he closed the door on her.

The visions finally slowed and settled into a heavy, still darkness that mercifully pulled him into sleep.

But it soon shifted to a restless sleep. He tossed and turned and gradually became aware of a

tiny noise. He desperately wanted to sleep, to forget, to sink into black nothingness, but the sound
kept waking him.

He lifted his head to listen. It sounded like a
child's soft weeping. He sat up, and realized it was
the boy. Drooms repented his cruel words; he could
never willingly hurt a child. He hoped the weeping
would stop. But it went on.

The sadness and pain that shaped the crying
left Drooms shaken. He couldn't take it anymore.

"Shhhh. I'm sorry boy. Don't cry. I'm sorry.
Please don't cry anymore."

But the heartrending sobs continued. Drooms
got up and looked for the boy.

He searched around his bedroom. Nothing
there. Then he saw that the door was open to the
inner room.

"Little boy? Where are you? Don't cry. Please
come back – it's not too late. Come back."

He looked inside the inner room, but it was
empty. He went into the living room and peered
around in the faint light. He could make out the
furniture, but he couldn't see the boy and he became
worried.

Then the weeping stopped, just a soft catching
of breath now. No, no – silence was always worse.

"Little boy? I'm so sorry. Please come back."

Drooms stumbled around his desk, the
couch. He walked towards the animal collection

on the bookshelves – then a flood of relief to see the boy standing there. Drooms almost laughed with joy. Of course the boy would be there, with the animals.

How could he have hurt him?

"Little boy, I'm so sorry –" But as Drooms reached out to touch him, he recoiled as his hand touched the stiff body. The boy had become stuffed like the animals, his face the last to change, tears still streaming down his cheeks.

Drooms backed up in horror, falling to the floor. He reached out again, only to pull back in revulsion.

"Oh, what have I done? Please come back! Oh, my God," he moaned, "what have I done?"

Drooms sat up in bed, pale and sweaty from the nightmare. His heart hammered inside his chest, as if tiny fists pounded on it, sending the vibration up to his neck and temples. He held his head, and gasped for air, until his breathing calmed.

Though he knew it was just a dream, he got up and looked around. He had to be sure. The door to the inner room was closed. Thank God.

His breathing still ragged, he stumbled into the living room, and stood in the center of the room. It was softly illuminated by the streetlight, but he could see that it was still the same; nothing had changed. There were the stuffed animals, frozen, rigid.

For the first time, he was repulsed by them. He saw them for the dusty, dead things they were, staring back at him with lifeless, glassy eyes. He slowly shook his head. He was not going to do that to himself. He was not.

He threw open the living room window, cold air rushing in. He then stood in front of the shelves and beheld the lifeless menagerie. He shuddered as he grabbed a bunch of the stiff animals and threw them out the window into the falling snow, crying out, "No more! No more!" Back and forth from shelves to window, tossing and throwing them out until the shelves were bare.

The animals landed on the snow below – squirrels, birds, rabbits, snakes in strange embraces and chase scenes.

In the distance a garbage truck made its way in the darkness of early morning, picking up the trash and the odd discarded items of humanity.

"No more!" cried Drooms as he crumpled to the floor, his hands over his face, rocking on his knees. "No more!"

Anguish, long pent up, now claimed its right, its life, and flailed out in a frenzy of unpracticed expression. Long years of tears came gushing forth, tears of the boy, and tears of the man – tears for the guilt, the loss, the raw festering loneliness. Anguish released in long, twisted groans and messy, wrenching weeping by a man searching for some answer in the darkness, his beseeching hands held open, weighted with the figment of sorrow.

The mourning that had never been expressed, the regret for the emptiness of years, now burst forth, knocking down the layers of hardness, tumbling the harsh rocky façade, stripping away the protective exterior – until there was nothing left, but the man himself – bent over a cold, dark floor. Weeping, like a child.

Chapter 12

The next morning after breakfast, Lillian packed two tins of Christmas cookies. She was thankful that she and the boys had the week off. She desperately needed the time to finish up with her Christmas preparations and put her mind in order.

And the extra hours of sleep were a luxury that she needed this morning, after the terrible night. She had barely slept. She kept thinking of the cruel words from Charles, though some part of her refused to believe them.

In the middle of the night she had woken, dreaming of him as he was in the sketch – struggling, alone. He was trying to move through the snow but couldn't, and he was beginning to freeze, the icicles keeping him bound. Lillian thought of the drawing of the woman in the long gown standing next to him, with the flame flower cupped in her hands.

Lillian turned on the lamp, brought the sketch pad to her bed, and finished the drawing. She colored the woman in soft shades of warm rose and blue and gold, and let the colors seep into the gray world of the frozen Drooms, the icicles catching the gold of the flame.

Lillian studied the drawing and felt that it was now complete. Then even though she believed that all doors between her and Charles were firmly closed, and that it was better this way, she had gotten out of bed, taken the drawing, and leaned it against his door.

She now wondered whether it was a drawing of the way things could have been, or the way things had actually been for a few beautiful moments. She frowned at her own thoughts. In the light of morning, it all seemed foolish.

She quickly dressed, powdered her strained and puffy face, and put on a cheerful front for the boys, who were dressed and ready for their visit to Santa.

"Come on, boys. We have a lot to do today. We'll deliver Mrs. Kuntzman's cookies on our way."

Gabriel had his coat on and could barely contain his excitement. "I'm gonna ask Santa for a sled, no – a puppy. No – a pirate sword!"

He cast a make-believe thrust at Tommy, who responded by unsheathing his own imaginary sword.

"Down villain! Bite the dust!" cried Tommy.

"Oh, yeah? Take this Peg Leg! Yaaargh!" Gabriel grabbed Tommy around the legs and they tumbled, laughing.

"Boys, boys! Come on now, we don't have time for that."

Lillian took one tin of cookies, and closed the door behind them. She glanced down the hall and saw that the drawing was still there, propped against Drooms's door. She briefly considered retrieving it, but the boys were already running down the stairs.

Gabriel gave a hearty Santa's laugh: "Ho ho ho!"

When Tommy answered in a pirate's voice, "And a bottle of rum," the boys doubled over in laughter.

They delivered the tin of cookies and spent a few minutes with Mrs. Kuntzman and her daughter, and then caught the bus to the department store.

Lillian looked out the bus window, wishing that she could go away for the week, to avoid bumping into him. Though it was last minute, perhaps she could take the boys upstate to her sister's for Christmas. Or maybe they could all take a trip somewhere.

No. It was no good running away from things. She would be fine. She would learn to think of him again as just a neighbor.

*

Spent, pummeled, exhausted, Drooms lay in a heavy, powerful, forgetting sleep. The blackness of nothingness reigned deep while the crumpled soul recovered and rested. A sleep that eventually grew into a lighter slumber as the soul healed and awoke.

Drooms rested in a state of soft waking, his mind rocking back and forth between dream images and awareness of his deep, rhythmic breathing. He lingered between sleep and waking, a kind of third place that he never knew existed, had always rushed by, never even catching a glimpse of it.

He savored the calm that pervaded him, wondering at the nightly miracle of sleep, the daily miracle of waking. Such a simple, pure thing, sleep. Like love, he thought. What a strange force is love – that lives beyond death, across time. His love for his mother, for Sarah and Sam was as strong today, was the same love, as it was back then. And he could still feel their love – nothing had changed or diminished.

And this new love, this new love that filled him –

His eyes snapped opened, and in a flash he saw Lillian's face, remembered his words to her, the sadness in her eyes. He whipped back the blanket. He could not let that look exist in the world, couldn't bear for her to feel pain, must hurry. He had to go to her.

Drooms saw the late time and dressed quickly. He recalled the nightmarish day and night, and still felt a sickness in his stomach when he thought of Gabriel lying in the snow.

But he no longer felt paralyzed, or immobilized by fear. He even wondered at the new feeling inside him, the light, effervescent feeling of hope. He would convince Lillian that he didn't mean any of it, that she was the best thing that had ever happened to him, and that he was grateful for her kindness and –

He wasn't sure what he would say, but he knew that what had happened between them was real and true and beautiful.

But perhaps it was too late, he thought. Perhaps all they could be now, after his terrible treatment of her, were friends, neighbors. He couldn't blame her for this.

No, however long it took, he would do what he could to make her life easier, to be there for her, to one day see that look of love and trust in her eyes again.

When he opened his door, he saw something propped against it. He lifted it and saw the drawing of him – it now had a woman in a flowing blue robe offering him warmth and light. His heart pounded; there was still hope.

Or, did the gesture mean that it was over – that this was what might have been? He felt a heavy darkness filling his chest at that possibility.

No, he would protect whatever remnant still remained. Gingerly, he held the drawing, searching for a safe place to put it. He went to his bedroom and laid it on his bed.

Then he left his apartment and knocked at Lillian's door. He had to know. He would know when he saw her face. He knocked again. Was she home and didn't want to see him? His despair deepened. He placed his hand on her door and spoke softly. "Lillian?"

Drooms saw the neighbor from the fourth floor coming up the stairs and, for a brief moment, was ready to scowl and leave. But that old self could not be summoned. Drooms actually smiled at the old man.

"Mrs. Hapsey and her boys left about an hour ago," the old man said. "Off to see Santa."

"Of course. Thank you. Merry Christmas."

The old man stood a moment, eyeing Drooms. "And a Merry Christmas to you, sir," and he continued up the stairs.

There's still hope, thought Drooms. He showered and dressed for work, with a clear vision of what he was going to do.

He ran down the stairs, and out into the fresh December air. He walked briskly with his head up, smiling and tipping his hat to the neighbors, which caused a few double takes.

When he passed The Red String Curio Store, he paused to look in the window at those combs. They did not have the same power they had yesterday. Today, they were just hair combs.

The shop owner knocked on the window and motioned for him to come in. Drooms smiled and opened the door, causing the little bell to jingle.

The owner was at his cheerful, holiday best. "Good morning, sir! I have a new raccoon you might like to take a look at. A nice addition to your collection."

"I got rid of that collection," said Drooms. "Decided to make room for other things."

"Oh. Well then," said the shopkeeper, clearly surprised. He hooked his thumbs around his red suspenders, rocking on his heels. "Can I help you find anything else?"

"I noticed some toys in the window," said Drooms.

"An excellent selection just delivered for Christmas."

After a few minutes, Drooms stacked several games and toys on the counter, smiling at the other customers.

"Can you wrap them, please? I'll pick them up in a few hours. Thank you. Merry Christmas!"

The shopkeeper chuckled lightly as the door closed. "There goes a man in love," he said, to no one in particular.

At Drooms Accounting, the staff discussed their plans for the holiday as they worked, all of them wondering at the fact that their boss was late. They broke up the merriment when Drooms hurried in.

For the first time, Drooms saw himself through their eyes, and the effect his presence had on them. He started to speak, but then went into his office, stopping Mrs. Murphy as she walked by.

"Mrs. Murphy, good morning. Please, call everyone together. I want to announce some changes." He saw the employees exchange nervous glances and make themselves busy at their desks.

"Oh, Mason. I want to speak to you first, in private. Please, come inside."

Drooms closed the door, took his seat, and gestured for Mason to sit down. He was puzzled when Mason remained standing.

Mason locked his hands in front of him and straightened, as if gathering strength for a battle.

"Before you begin, sir, I must speak my mind about the takeover."

Drooms cocked his head to the side, and knitted his eyebrows in confusion. "Takeover?" He then remembered his earlier intention that Mason referred to, and waved it away. "Oh, that. Bad idea. I've changed my mind. Henderson's a good man."

After a moment of surprise, Mason's shoulders relaxed somewhat. He looked down and put his hands on the back of the chair in front of him.

"Well then, I guess I know what this is about. Let me speak plainly. I know you're upset at my taking a second job. But I honestly don't believe it has affected my performance. However, if –"

Drooms jerked his head back at the preposterous idea. "I couldn't be more pleased with your work. Please, sit down, Mason."

Mason sat down hesitantly. "But – I thought when you gave the Carson account to Finch that you –"

Drooms's effervescence vanished for just a moment. "I thought you were leaving me, Mason. Going over to Henderson. I saw you two shaking hands."

Mason dropped his mouth open, searching his memory for when he had last seen Henderson, and then he remembered. "That was just a holiday wish of good cheer. Why would I leave?"

"Forgive me, Mason. I haven't quite been myself." Drooms didn't want to dwell in the past. He waved his hand again, as if brushing aside his old ways.

"Look. I know I'm not always the easiest person to work with, but I've been thinking things through and – well, I'm going to make you a partner."

Mason thought he must have misunderstood him. He shook his head lightly, and leaned forward, waiting for Drooms to repeat himself. "I'm sorry, I didn't hear –"

"Partner. I'm going to make you a partner."

Mason tried to read the unusual expression on Drooms's face. It seemed to be one of unbounded happiness.

Drooms had expected a different response and hoped he hadn't been presumptuous in thinking that Mason would want to be a partner with him. "That is, if you're interested."

"Partner? I don't know what to say. Of course! A partner?" Mason's expression bounced back and forth between confusion and joy.

"It's long overdue. I'm only sorry I didn't realize it earlier." Drooms handed him an envelope. "Here's your bonus, Mason." He waited as Mason sat speechless. "Well, open it."

Mason opened the envelope and was overcome with emotion. Inside was the end to his immediate financial pressures, and a brief vision of himself as he presented his wife with the new coat she had so admired. He stood up. "Excuse me, sir," but his voice broke. He held up a finger. "A moment, please." He left the room to compose himself, and stepped out into the hall.

The other employees saw Mason leave Drooms's office visibly shaken, holding an envelope. They kept their heads down, eyes on their desks, afraid of what was coming next.

Drooms stood in his doorway and cheerfully called Mrs. Murphy. "Please, step inside."

An angry Mrs. Murphy, who had also witnessed the distraught departure of Mason, stomped into Drooms's office and shut the door behind her, not waiting for him to speak.

"Mr. Drooms. In all my years I have never spoken out against you, but if you have gone and fired your best employee, after all these years –"

"Fire Mason? Why would I do that? No. I've made him a partner."

She covered her mouth, and her eyes crinkled with happiness, and then began to fill with tears.

"And I'm giving you a well-deserved raise, starting with this bonus," he said, pressing the envelope into her hand.

She stared at the envelope, opened it, and gasped. She tried twice to speak, pulled a hankie from her sleeve and dabbed her eyes. Then, like Mason, she left the room to compose herself.

The staff stared in disbelief.

Drooms saw their expressions and came out.

"This isn't going as planned. This isn't what I had in mind. Wait. Just a moment."

He stepped outside the office and gestured Mason and Mrs. Murphy back in. "I'm going to need your help with this."

He then addressed all of them, with Mason and Mrs. Murphy standing on either side of him.

"Now, gather round, please. The changes I was referring to are good changes. We're a good team and we're going to be even better," he said, placing an arm around Mason, "with Mason here as partner. The firm will henceforth be called Drooms and Mason."

After a moment of astonishment, they broke into a round of happy congratulations. Drooms shook their hands as he handed out envelopes.

"Here are your Christmas bonuses. I couldn't be more pleased with you. Now, you should all be home with your families. Go. We're finished here."

Amid wishes of "Merry Christmas," "Thank you, sir," and "God bless you," they excitedly gathered their coats and hats.

Drooms called out to them as they left, "And don't come back until the New Year!"

As Mason prepared to leave, Drooms walked over to him and patted him on the back.

"Give my regards to your wife, your family, Mason. By the way, how are the twins? They must be nearly five now."

Mason smiled. "Almost ten. Doing very well. Thank you, sir. Merry Christmas."

Drooms left the office, and enjoyed the bustle as he walked along Fifth Avenue. So many happy people everywhere.

When he passed the Salvation Army bell ringer, he took out his wallet, folded some bills, and stuffed them in the bucket. He tipped his hat to the carolers on the corner and wished them a Merry Christmas.

He looked up at the sunny blue sky, at the snow piled along the sidewalk, and rubbed his hands together as if for warmth, but in truth, it was in excitement. Life, he thought, is richer and deeper when there is love in your heart.

Drooms made his way to a side street and searched for a store he had passed not long ago. There it was, an art supply store. Its windows were decked with pine garlands and colored lights, reminding him of the night he and Lillian had set up her tree. He gazed at the display of beautiful wooden boxes full of assorted paints, pencils, and crayons.

Fifteen minutes later, Drooms left the store carrying a large flat box tied in red ribbon. He made his way home in a hurry, all the while telling himself, It can't be too late. I won't let it be.

*

Lillian and the boys returned late in the afternoon. As they mounted the stairs, Lillian saw that the drawing outside Drooms's door was gone. It was as if another version of herself had placed it there, in the overwrought emotional spikes of the night. She would give it no more thought. He was a closed man, whatever his reasons. And just as well. She was better off alone.

The boys had two little bags of oranges and hard Christmas candy. Gabriel started to run towards Drooms's apartment. "I want to give Mr. Drooms some candy."

"Yeah, let's show Mr. Drooms what we got," said Tommy.

"No, come inside, boys. You can hang the candy canes on the tree. Come, help me get dinner ready."

She ushered them inside and turned on the lamps. The boys placed their things on the coffee table, stepped out of their stiff shoes, and peeled off their coats.

"Get out of your good clothes." As they ran into their bedroom, she called after them. "And put them away nicely!"

When the phone rang, her pulse quickened and blood rushed to her face. She frowned that her heart had not kept pace with her mind's decision. But it was Izzy on the line, asking if Lillian could run downstairs for just a moment. She and Red were on their way and wanted to stop by to wish her a Merry Christmas.

After she hung up, Lillian set out a fruit cake for Izzy and a tin of cookies for Red. She gazed out the kitchen window at the fading day. Across the way, golden light poured from the windows of the apartments, spilling onto the snow-filled ledges. A few windows revealed Christmas trees, some already lit for the evening. On the sidewalk below, a group of children were putting the finishing touches on a snowman, adding a carrot nose and stick arms. People were coming and going from the apartments; a mother stood in a doorway, calling her children in from play.

Lillian began to prepare dinner. She put a crocheted tablecloth over the table, and in the center placed the sugar-dusted gingerbread with a sprig of holly on top. She then turned on the oven and put in a casserole she had made the day before. As she took out some vegetables and began to wash them, she mentally made sure she had everything for Christmas dinner the next day.

The boys emerged in their day clothes. Gabriel ran to the kitchen and impulsively hugged her. "I love you, Mommy!"

Tommy also hugged her. "Me too, Mommy!"

Lillian's hands were full with wet vegetables, but she embraced them both. "My boys!"

Tommy picked up the box of candy canes from the table. "Can we hang them?"

"Yes," said Lillian. "And let's have some Christmas music."

Tommy turned on the radio, and dramatically mimicked the crooning. Gabriel joined him and they tumbled onto the couch laughing. They opened the box of candy canes and began hanging them on the tree.

A few minutes later a horn tooted twice. Lillian went to the window and saw Izzy and Red standing next to a cab. She waved at them and motioned that she would come down.

"I'll be right back, boys." She put on her sweater and took the fruit cake and tin of cookies.

When Lillian saw Izzy and Red, she was struck by how happy they seemed. She handed Red the tin, and the fruitcake to Izzy.

"Your famous fruitcake?" asked Izzy.

Lillian nodded. "My mother's recipe."

Izzy elbowed Red. "It's loaded with brandy – delicious!" She turned to Lillian. "Thanks, Lilly. We'll have it tomorrow. Red is having Christmas with me."

Red reached into the taxi and handed a bag to Lillian. "Merry Christmas!"

She saw that inside was a bottle tied with a ribbon around it and two giftwrapped boxes.

"Games for the boys – from me and Red," Izzy said, as she linked her arm with Red.

"You didn't have to," said Lillian, "but thank you. The boys will be so pleased." She looked at the presents and imagined them under the tree. They would help to fill in the gaps. "They're opening their presents tonight. Thank you, Red. Thanks, Izzy."

Lillian looked from Izzy to Red who kept exchanging glances, and squeezing each other's hand.

Red finally nudged Izzy and laughed. "Go ahead. Tell her!"

Izzy took off her glove and held up her hand, displaying a ring.

Lillian gasped at the news. "Engaged?"

"Red leaves end of next month. We're getting married before he goes."

Red threw his arm around Izzy and kissed her cheek. "I'm the luckiest fellow in the world!" He lifted her for a second in sheer exuberance and kissed her again, then gave Lillian a kiss on the cheek.

Lillian laughed at the joy they couldn't contain. "That's wonderful news! I'm so happy for you both." She took Izzy's hand and admired the ring. "It's beautiful." Her voice quivered as she spoke and she felt tears in her eyes. She tried to laugh her emotions away, but by then Izzy was also starting to cry.

Red took over. "No time for that. This is supposed to be a happy day."

Izzy laughed and dabbed her eyes and gave Lillian a quick hug. "Well, we gotta run. We're making the rounds. Merry Christmas, Lilly!"

"Merry Christmas! Take good care of yourself, Red."

Lillian waved goodbye as they climbed into the taxi. She laughed when Red planted a big exaggerated kiss on Izzy's cheek.

Lillian watched the red tail lights disappear around the corner with the happy couple inside. She held her sweater close. Dusk had now settled on the sidewalk, on the row of brownstones.

She looked down the street, empty and quiet now. Mounds of snow lay on the edge of the sidewalk and in between the cars. Some cars had never been dug out, and remained white mounds with black showing through where the kids had knocked off the snow. She gazed up at the dark sky and slowly walked back inside.

*

While Lillian was downstairs, there was a knock at the door. Gabriel was at the window where he saw Lillian take the gift from Red. Now he raced Tommy to the door and shrieked with delight to see Drooms standing there with presents stacked in his arms.

"Hi, Mr. Drooms!" His eyes opened wide.

"Wow! Presents!" said Tommy.

Gabriel gave him a big hug. "I knew you would come! Are these for us?"

Drooms laughed as he handed them the presents. "Of course, they're for you."

The boys ran to put them under the tree. Drooms looked around for Lillian. "Is your mother here?"

"She's downstairs kissing that man who gave her a present," Gabriel said.

Drooms stood staring, as if he didn't quite understand. Then his smile slowly disappeared. What had he been thinking? Why had he been so hopeful, so happy? There must be some mistake. He bunched his eyebrows together, and focused on the floor, as if searching for something.

"Don't be a dope, Gabe. She won't be long, Mr. Drooms. Come on in."

Drooms started to leave. The last thing he wanted to see was Lillian with someone else.

"No, no, I just wanted to say Merry Christmas. I have to go. I'll see you later, boys."

Tommy stood looking after him, once again disappointed at his sudden departure.

Drooms quickly closed the door. He stood a moment in the hallway, and then leaned his head against her door. The sense of loss overwhelmed him. Her smile, her walk, her voice, had already become a part of him.

He felt his heart beating at the words that were forming in his mind. "I love her," he whispered.

But then she was so loveable, of course others must feel the same way. How could they not? He ran several scenarios through his mind, thinking Gabriel must be mistaken. Yet neither boy had seemed surprised by her actions. Perhaps she had someone all along. Perhaps there was something between her and Rockwell. And why shouldn't she have someone, someone who would treat her well and –

He turned quickly and saw Lillian coming up the last flight of stairs, carrying a bag.

He glared and looked behind her for someone else, listened for another set of footsteps.

Lillian was surprised to see him standing outside her door. She glanced behind her to see who he was looking for, and then back to Drooms.

"Isn't your friend coming?" he asked.

Lillian stopped, perplexed. "No. Why?"

"The boys said you were downstairs kissing a man." There. He had thrown down the gauntlet. He didn't care if he sounded petty or jealous. He had to know where he stood.

A slow smile spread across Lillian's face, and she felt herself grow warm as a jolt of life coursed through her. She didn't want him to see that she was blushing, so she kept her head down and climbed the last few steps. She could almost laugh out loud at the thoughts that ran through her mind. Did he really think she had someone else? Was that jealousy in his voice? In a flash she knew that nothing had changed between them. A little scar tissue that would fade with time, nothing more.

She stood before him. Behind her fears, and trying to convince herself that she wanted to be alone, she knew it was too late. There was the man she loved. Difficult, contrary, wounded – there he was with that look in his eyes, so much passion and vulnerability locked inside him. She couldn't prolong his anguish any longer.

"My friend, Izzy, and her beau. We exchanged gifts," she said, setting the bag down.

Drooms slowly closed his eyes and felt like an absolute fool. But when he opened them, he saw love in her eyes.

Lillian held his gaze, controlled his gaze, as she waited for him to explain his behavior. She had made up her mind about him, and loved him as he was, but she wanted to be equally sure of his feelings for her.

Drooms placed a hand on her shoulder. "Lillian. I'm so sorry for yesterday, for what I said. You know I didn't mean it." When she didn't say anything, he took her hand. "Please tell me I'm not too late."

He lifted her face and searched her eyes for an answer.

Though she wanted to throw her arms around him, she forced herself to remain still, and to speak calmly. "I don't think you're sure about how you feel."

"I've never been more sure about anything. Please give me the chance to show you." He took both her hands. "I – I want to explain something to you. I want you to know why...why I – why I over-reacted when I thought Gabriel was hurt." He bent his head down and found that he didn't know how to start, where to start. He swallowed hard. "I..., I – When I was –"

Lillian placed a hand on his arm. "That's all right, Charles." She couldn't bear to see him struggling with his pain. "You don't have to tell me now."

The tenderness in her voice as she spoke his name, the light touch on his arm, was like balm to him. He put his hand to her soft cheek and knew that everything would be all right.

Just then the door flung open and Tommy poked his head into the hall. "Mom! Look what Mr. Drooms brought us."

Gabriel ran up next to Tommy. "Mommy, he brought presents! They're under the tree!"

Lillian smiled and took Drooms by the hand. "Well, let's take a look! Come in, Charles."

He followed her in, never taking his eyes off her.

The boys ran to the tree and held up the presents, talking and stumbling over each other in their excitement. Tommy held up the large box tied with red ribbon and read the tag. "Hey, this one is for you, Mom!" The boys whooped as they shook presents and arranged them under the tree.

Lillian reached to kiss Drooms on the cheek. "You'll join us for dinner?"

Drooms nodded and ran his hand over her hair and rested it gently on her shoulder.

Lillian smiled at their unspoken pact. "Boys, show Mr. Drooms the tree while I finish getting dinner ready."

The boys pulled Drooms over to the tree. Gabriel handed him the box of candy canes.

"Here, Mr. Drooms, you can hang the high ones. And I'll hang the low ones. Oops." He began to eat the candy cane he just broke, and offered some to Drooms and Tommy.

Lillian cast frequent glances at Drooms, just as he watched her moving about the kitchen.

They both started when they heard Tommy's panicked voice. "Oh, no! Mom!"

A worried look crossed her face. "Now what?"

"We forgot to get a star!"

Gabriel became equally worried. "We have to have something at the top, Mommy. Otherwise it won't really be finished."

Lillian stood with the silverware in her hands. "I completely forgot."

Both boys were alarmed at not having a completed tree. Gabriel looked from Tommy to Lillian to Drooms, waiting for someone to solve the problem. He then hit on an idea. "Can we borrow your star, Mr. Drooms?"

Drooms was about to explain that he didn't have any decorations, when he suddenly remembered the boxes of old family things his sister Kate had sent years ago. He had completely forgotten about them. He was sure there were some Christmas decorations in them.

"Boys, Mr. Drooms doesn't have anything. We'll just have to do without one this year."

"I can't say for sure," said Drooms, "but I think I might have something – packed away."

Lillian stood in amazement. "Really?"

"I think so." He turned to the boys. "Shall we go and see if I'm right? We might have to dig through a few boxes."

Tommy raised his eyebrows. "Can we Mom?" Gabriel had already run to the door and was jumping up and down.

"Yes. Go and help Mr. Drooms," said Lillian.

The boys ran ahead. "Hurry, Mr. Drooms!"

He laughed at their excitement, and hoped he was correct in his recollection. It was so long since he had thought about those boxes.

He opened the door to his apartment and went to the inner room. The boys looked up at him as he hesitated a moment, his hand on the doorknob. Then he opened it and switched on the light. It was just a dark closet full of old stuff that needed cleaning out. Nothing more. He shifted the old files and dusty boxes around, and then lifted a box from the top shelf.

"It's somewhere in here. In one of these large boxes, I think. Here, Tommy. You start on this one." He set down a box outside the room for Tommy to search through, and then took down another box, and he and Gabriel began rummaging through it.

Gabriel identified the items he pulled out. "Letters. Photos. Papers."

Tommy soon cried out in surprise. "Hey! Look! I think I found it!" He pulled out a beautiful, intricate silver star.

Drooms smiled and nodded at his find.

"Wait till Mom sees this!" Tommy ran off, yelling, "Mom! I found it!"

In the same box where Tommy found the star, Drooms noticed a box of old glass ornaments. He recognized them all – St. Nicholas holding a tree, the little houses and churches, the shiny trumpets and glittering drums. He carefully lifted the box and brought it to Gabriel.

Just inside the inner room, Gabriel was looking at a tiny old photograph of a mischievous looking boy who was smiling, with a scarf around his neck.

"Hey," said Gabriel. "Who's this?"

Drooms took the photograph and brushed off the dust. He smiled as he beheld the tiny photo.

"That's me," he said softly. "When I was a boy."

Gabriel saw the box of ornaments and gasped when he spotted the red Santa holding a Christmas tree. "I can't believe it! Just like my ornament. Can I show Mommy?"

Drooms laughed. "Yes. Let's hang them all on the tree."

Gabriel ran back to his apartment, crying, "Mommy! Look! You won't believe what I found! My Santa ornament!"

Drooms looked again at the photo that had been taken just a few weeks before the accident. He saw the young face with the impish smile, the hope and happiness in the eyes – and he was grateful to know that something of that younger self dwelled in him still.

He placed the photo back in the box and closed the door. And with some of that little-boy lightness back in his step, he returned to Lillian, and to life.